"You have to help me, Noah. *He's still out there...*"

"He tried to kidnap me." Rachel's voice was little more than a hoarse whisper, the words shocking.

"Who's out there?" Noah whirled to look in the direction she pointed, then back at her.

"I don't know who he is. He had on a mask and it was dark. He came into my home and tried to force me to go with him."

Through the headlights, he could see red marks on her cheek. Her bare feet were cut and bloody, hands scraped, her flame-red hair loose and tangled.

"Let's get you inside the cruiser where it's warm. You must be frozen." When she seemed incapable of putting one foot in front of the other, he clasped her arm and gently guided her to the passenger side.

Her stricken gaze locked on to him, and he knew something else was coming. "Noah, I think he has Eva."

"What do you mean he has Eva?"

"She wasn't in her room and her bed was not slept in. He has her, Noah. You have to find my sister."

Mary Alford was inspired to become a writer after reading romantic suspense greats Victoria Holt and Phyllis A. Whitney. Soon, creating characters and throwing them into dangerous situations that tested their faith came naturally for Mary. In 2012 Mary entered the speed-dating contest hosted by Love Inspired Suspense and later received "the call." Writing for Love Inspired Suspense has been a dream come true for Mary.

Books by Mary Alford

Love Inspired Suspense

Forgotten Past
Rocky Mountain Pursuit
Deadly Memories
Framed for Murder
Standoff at Midnight Mountain
Grave Peril
Amish Country Kidnapping

Visit the Author Profile page at Harlequin.com.

AMISH COUNTRY KIDNAPPING

MARY ALFORD

HARLEQUIN® LOVE INSPIRED® SUSPENSE

Recycling programs
for this product may
not exist in your area.

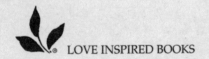

LOVE INSPIRED BOOKS

ISBN-13: 978-1-335-40255-4

Amish Country Kidnapping

www.Harlequin.com

Printed in U.S.A.

So teach us to number our days,
that we may apply our hearts unto wisdom.
–*Psalm* 90:12

To my husband, Monte, who is my biggest supporter, in both writing and in life. You are a true blessing from God and I love you so much.

Success in marriage is not only finding the right person, it is being the right person.
—an Amish proverb

Monte, you are definitely the right person for me.

Acknowledgments

Lord Jesus, let the words of my mouth and the meditations of my heart always be pleasing to You.

To my granddaughters, Ava, Makinze and Baylee. You are all so special to me and my heart is filled with happiness just to see your smiling faces. I love you all so much.

To each member of Mary's Book Crew. Your support means so much to me. You are all dynamos and awesome ladies. A true dream team. I am so grateful to have each of you on my side.

To my agent, Rachel Kent, who has been there for me through the good, the bad and all my wild questions in between. Thank you!

To Ann Ellison. You were always such a positive influence and a strong Texas lady. I miss your support, but our loss here on earth is Heaven's gain.

To Cheryl Baranski. You were such a wonderful example of what a true warrior of God should look like. I know God is thrilled to have you home.

ONE

Breathe! The disjointed thought sped through Rachel Albrecht's mind. Her eyes snapped open. She struggled to draw enough air into her lungs. Something covered her mouth and nose. Her heart accelerated as she glanced around the familiar bedroom she once shared with her husband, unable to understand what was happening.

Her last memory was of falling asleep in her favorite chair reading the Bible while waiting for her sister, Eva, to return.

Now darkness flooded the room. The lantern's wick had gone out.

Through the pitch-black of night the truth became horrifying. A strange man towered above her, his big gloved hand covering part of her face. She clawed at it as the last bit of air left her body.

He leaned in close, his face completely obscured by a ski mask, only his eyes visible. They burned into hers, the evil filling them chilling.

"You're coming with me," he growled, then removed his hand and hauled her from the chair. The Bible fell to the floor at her feet.

Air rushed into her lungs and she coughed, her eyes filling with tears as she continued to drag in breaths.

"Let's go," he ordered and pointed to the door. He shoved something against her side. A gun! The sight of it promised all sorts of unwelcome outcomes. She needed help.

His hot breath fanned across her cheek, his big body blocking her path to the door. If she could make it to the closet, Daniel's old shotgun was stored there. Though her husband never kept the weapon loaded, she knew where the bullets were and could use the gun to defend herself.

Breaking free, she ran for the closet, her heart echoing in her ears. Rachel barely managed a couple of steps before his hand snaked around her shoulder. She lost her balance and sprawled across the floor.

"Oh no, you don't," he snarled. Grabbing a handful of her loose hair, he hauled her to her feet. Pieces of hair were ripped from her scalp. Rachel screamed, frantically scratching at his arms, his chest, anything to free herself.

He jerked her against his body and smacked her hard with his open hand. "That's for trying to get away from me. You've wasted enough of my time. Now, let's go."

His hand clutched her arm tight. The gun bit into her ribs.

With all her strength, she tried to twist free, but his grip tightened, fingers digging into her arm.

"Eva, run!" Rachel yelled as loud as she could, thinking only of her seventeen-year-old sister asleep in the bedroom next to hers.

"Keep your mouth shut and do as I say," he snapped and forced her toward the door.

Please, Gott, help me... The frantic prayer slipped through her head as she did her best to drag her feet. She'd need His help if she was going to survive this attack. Her homestead was isolated on the outskirts of the Amish community of West Kootenai, Montana. The Beacheys, her closest neighbors, were almost a mile away. No one would be coming to her aid. Her survival was in *Gott*'s hands…and her own.

"Move! *He* has plans for you," the man barked when she continued to dig her heels in. His words were terrifying. This was not a random attack. She'd been purposefully targeted.

With a strength she could only believe was sent from *Gott*, she snatched at his mask with her free hand.

Uttering a string of disgusting words, he released his hold on her arm and tried to capture her flailing hand. The mask ripped free. With morning still hours away, shadows clung to everything in the room. The man's frightening eyes were the only thing that stood out in her mind. She would never forget them as long as she lived.

Eva. She had to find a way to save her sister.

The man smacked her hard once more, then yanked her close, his clawlike grip bruising her upper arm through her nightgown.

Rachel could not envision the fate waiting for her if he took her.

Trying to remain calm was next to impossible. With only one option left, Rachel slumped against him with her eyes closed. He seized her by the shoulders to keep her from falling.

"What's wrong with you?" he asked with just enough uncertainty to make her believe he'd bought her act. This was her only chance. She slammed her bare foot against his shin as hard as she could. He yelped in pain and clutched his injured leg.

Freed, Rachel shoved him hard. Caught unawares, the man stumbled to the floor, taking the table holding the dark lantern with him.

She didn't look back as she raced for the door. Behind her, another string of bad words was followed by the noise of furniture being shoved out of the way. He was coming after her!

"Eva, wake up!" she screamed. How could Eva sleep through such noise?

Reaching Eva's open door, the bed appeared still made from the morning. Eva never came home. Terror threatened to stop her dead. Had the man already taken her sister?

Her pursuer slammed against the adjoining wall. She had seconds to escape. With her sister's well-being foremost in her thoughts, Rachel reached the front door. Her fingers shook so much it was a struggle to turn the knob. She yanked the door open and clicked the lock on the knob before slamming it closed.

Her bare feet hit the front porch. She cleared the steps, stumbling across the frozen ground. To her left: the wheat field Thomas Beachey planted for her, the tender shoots still inching their way above ground. To her right: a patch of woods before the road that separated her place from her neighbors'. Rachel turned right and ran toward the neighbors' place.

Fresh-fallen snow blanketed the countryside. Winter might have been months away in most of the States, but in the big sky country of Montana, it already held the countryside in its icy clutches.

With her lungs burning from the cold, Rachel ran as fast as her bare feet would allow. She had to reach the Beacheys.

Behind her, the door flew open and slammed against the wall. "Where do you think you're going? There's no one here to help you," the man shouted, his anger emphasizing each word.

Her steps hiccupped. *Gott, keep my faith strong in You.* She would not give in to the fear. Eva needed her.

With her feet growing numb, fallen trees tore at her tender flesh. Close by, her attacker entered the woods. His labored breathing made it sound as if he were right on top of her. Ignoring the pain, Rachel gathered her dwindling energy and kept running.

Up above, the clouds covered the moon and stars. In the deep woods, the darkness was so intense she could barely see her hand in front of her.

Branches snapped as the man plowed through the trees behind her. These woods were as familiar to her as the back of her hand. She had the advantage.

In front of her, the woods thinned. Almost there. The path blurred with her tears. What did this man want?

The road appeared before her. Across it, the Beacheys' house loomed as a shadow, save a single light burning in the kitchen. Someone was awake.

Rachel stumbled onto the road. Losing her footing on the icy pavement, she fell hard to her knees. *Please, no.* Not like this. Not without knowing her sister's fate.

Frantic, she glanced back. A dark silhouette appeared at the edge of the woods. The man spotted her and started running toward her.

"Help!" she screamed as loud as her labored voice would allow, hoping the Beacheys might hear her. "Help me, please!"

With scraped hands, she pushed off the pavement and managed to keep her feet underneath her. Hurry. She had to. But it was impossible on the slick road.

She peeked over her shoulder. The man had stopped near the road. He was no longer looking at her but down the road. What was he waiting for?

Beyond her drumming heartbeat, she caught the sound of a car's engine coming toward her. Rachel whirled at the sound. The vehicle topped the hill close by. Blinding headlights pinned her in place. Before she had time to react, the SUV was almost on top of her.

What if the driver worked with her attacker? She'd fought so hard to be free only to die here on this road.

Tires squealed on the slick road as the driver tried to stop before he hit her. Rachel shielded her eyes against the glare. Her heart in her throat, she braced for the impact.

Seconds passed. Nothing happened. Quiet returned to the countryside. The car had stopped. She was alive. A single breath slipped from her body. Her gaze darted to the last place she'd seen her attacker. He wasn't there.

The Beacheys' home was close. If she ran, would she make it in time?

The SUV's door opened. Her heartbeat ticked the seconds off.

"Rachel?" That voice! It jumped out at her from her youthful past. Noah? More than seven years had passed since he'd moved away, yet she'd thought of him so often through the years. The young man she'd lost her heart to at seventeen had now just saved her life.

Deputy Sheriff Noah Warren wasn't sure he trusted his eyes. Standing before him, illuminated by the bright headlights of his patrol vehicle, was the woman who'd stolen his eighteen-year-old heart.

And he'd broken hers.

As he advanced on her, the shock of seeing Rachel again under these unexpected conditions sent shock waves through his body.

"Rachel?" he said her name again and blinked, half expecting her to disappear. When he opened his eyes, she was still there and one thing became clear—the look of fear on her face appeared permanently embedded there.

Her green eyes were huge pools of light that told a story of desperation.

Noah couldn't believe his past mistakes were about to reach out to him once more. He'd thought of her so many times through the years, considered reaching out to her when the heartaches of her life took place. Thought better of it. He'd hurt her badly. She wouldn't welcome hearing from him again after the way things ended. Best to leave the past where it lay. As hard as it was to accept, their future was never intended to be together. God had other plans for both of them.

He snapped out of his daze. "Are you hurt?" he asked, his voice anything but steady, reflecting how he felt.

Rachel took an involuntary step back and peeked over her shoulder. Shivered visibly.

"You have to help me, Noah. He's still out there. He tried to kidnap me." Her voice was little more than a hoarse whisper, the words shocking.

Noah whirled to look in the direction she pointed, then back at her. "Who's out there?"

"I don't know who he is. He wore a mask and it was dark. He came into my home and tried to force me to go with him."

Noah couldn't believe what he heard. Through the headlights, he could see red marks on her cheek. Her bare feet were cut and bloody, hands scraped, flame-red hair loose and tangled.

"Let's get you inside the cruiser where it's warm. You must be frozen." When she seemed incapable of moving, he clasped her arm and gently guided her to the passenger side.

Opening the door, he paused when Rachel didn't budge. Her stricken gaze locked onto him, and he knew something else was coming.

"Noah, I think he has Eva."

The news robbed him of his next breath. "What do you mean he has Eva?"

"She wasn't in her room and her bed was not unmade. Eva promised to be home by ten and she wouldn't break that promise. He has her, Noah. You have to find my sister."

Eva missing? He still remembered the young blonde girl who used to follow them around. "I'll find her, I promise. Come, get inside where it's warm. I need to call for backup." The urgency in his tone must have reached through her fear. Gathering the skirt of her gown, she climbed inside. Noah retrieved the blanket he kept in the SUV along with other emergency supplies and tucked it around her legs. Clicking the locks in place, he shut the door and reached for the radio attached to his jacket.

In the distance, a vehicle fired to life. Noah swung toward the sound. It sounded close, a little ways past Rachel's home. He peered into the dark night. No lights appeared. Had he been wrong about the distance? Noises carried in the country, the sound echoing off the mountains. Perhaps the car was farther down the road than he thought. As much as he wanted to investigate, he didn't dare leave Rachel alone.

"Dispatch, this is Deputy Warren requesting immediate backup for a possible 207 on Spruce Road near the Beachey farm."

The sheriff's dispatcher, Janine Mills, picked up right away. "Copy that, Noah." A second of silence followed. "Aden and Megan are en route. I'll notify the sheriff. Is anyone hurt? Do you need an ambulance?"

He glanced inside the patrol vehicle where Rachel watched him with huge eyes. "Yes, send a bus. The victim has cuts on her feet and she's been exposed to the cold for a while. It would be a good idea to have an EMT take a look at her."

"Will do. Backup is five minutes out. Stay safe, Noah."

Noah ended the transmission and called Aden on his cell.

"We're close," Aden assured him.

"Good. Can you and Megan take a quick ride down Aspen Glen Road? I heard a car start up a little distance from here. It might be nothing."

"Or it could be our perp. We're at the intersection now. Talk to you soon."

Noah shoved the phone in his pocket and clicked on his flashlight, moving to the edge of the road. He flashed the light in the direction of Rachel's childhood home. Her bare footprints were in the snow along with a second, much larger, shoed set of prints. His gut told him the noise he'd heard was the perp escaping down the road that ran in front of Rachel's home. There were numerous back roads intersecting Aspen Glen. The man could be anywhere.

He'd knelt to examine the prints when voices carried his way. Noah rose and spun toward the sound. Two people hurried his way, guided by the light of a lantern. He recognized Thomas and Jane Beachey immediately. They must have heard his vehicle.

Not knowing if Rachel's attacker was working alone, Noah sought to warn the older couple. "Thomas, I need you and Jane to return to your house right away. Lock your doors. I'll explain later." Thomas hesitated before gathering Jane close. With another troubled glance behind him, Thomas urged Jane toward the house.

Noah opened the SUV door and climbed in beside Rachel. Even visibly shaken she was still as pretty as he remembered. When he looked at her, all the things he'd once hoped for came to mind. A simple life with her as his wife. Children of their own. Things his father's interference had robbed them of.

"I know this is hard, but I need to you tell me everything that happened tonight."

She rubbed her hands down her arms, probably to ward off more than just the chill of the night. Noah cranked the heater up a couple notches while Rachel told him about waking up to find a stranger standing over her. "He had a gun, Noah. He pointed it at my side and forced me to go with him." She gestured toward her left side. "He said, 'He has plans for you.' I have no idea what he meant by that. His face was covered with a ski mask and he had on gloves."

The attack was planned. Deliberate. Confusing. Why would someone wish to harm either Rachel or Eva? It didn't add up in his mind.

"We struggled. I managed to rip the mask off, but it was so dark. I couldn't see anything…except his eyes." She shuddered visibly. "I will never forget those dark, angry eyes for as long as I live."

He clasped her hand, and she turned to face him. The extent of what she'd gone through showed in her drawn expression. All he wanted to do was take her in his arms and reassure her everything would be okay. Yet he couldn't lie to her.

On the hill behind him, red-and-blue lights strobed in the starless night. A patrol vehicle, sirens blaring, blasted down Spruce Road. The vehicle slid to a halt when the driver spotted his cruiser in the middle of the road.

"I'll be right back," he told her. When she didn't respond, Noah climbed out and hurried to his colleagues. Aden Scott exited his vehicle first, followed by Deputy Megan Clark.

"Sheriff's on his way. Ambo is five minutes out. We drove a good way down Aspen Glen, but there was no sign of a vehicle. What do you have here?" Aden pointed to the cruiser where Rachel waited inside.

Noah outlined the few details he knew so far. He shined the light on the ground where retreating footsteps appeared to be heading through the woods the same way they'd come. "I heard a car's engine start up a few minutes after I spotted Rachel. If it was him, he's long gone."

Aden nodded. "Let's hope not. We'll follow the footprints and see what we can find."

Clicking on their flashlights, both Aden and Megan started out.

Noah went back to the vehicle. Rachel stared straight ahead, showing obvious signs of shock. Her shoulders hunched defensively. She'd never looked so vulnerable before. Growing up, Rachel had always been fearless. Seeing her as a victim now just wouldn't compute with what he knew about her.

He'd give anything to ease her pain, but he had a feeling this was just the beginning.

"There's an ambulance on the way. They'll need to examine your injuries."

Her huge green eyes found him. "I am fine, Noah. I do not need an ambulance."

"You do," he insisted. "You have some nasty cuts on your feet. Not to mention those scrapes on your face." Anger rose to the surface when he spotted what appeared to a flamed impression of a handprint on her cheek.

I think he has Eva... Rachel's words haunted him, as did her fear.

"Why do you think he took Eva?" he asked because his brain was working overtime searching for answers. "She's going through her *rumspringa*, correct? Is it possible the time got away from her and she stayed with a friend?"

Rachel didn't let him finish. "*Nay*, Eva told me she would be home by ten and she wouldn't be late. Not now."

"Why not?" he asked, curious about her response.

"Because Eva has been training with Hannah Wagler to take over as the community teacher in a few weeks' time. She loves her students and wanted to get a *gut* night's rest to be prepared for them. They are very important to her. She's missing, Noah. I know she is." Her answer wiped away the last of his doubts. They'd need to speak with the last person who saw Eva, and soon.

"Tell me what happened yesterday. Did anything unusual take place? What were Eva's plans for the day?" He couldn't imagine anything bad happening to the little girl he once knew so well.

Rachel swallowed visibly. "Nothing unusual. Eva and I rode to church service together. It began around nine. Afterward, there was the church meal. I said goodbye to her around three. She planned to attend the youth group singing. Afterward, she was going home with her friend, Anna Lapp. She said she would walk home after spending time with Anna. Eva was excited about the following *shool* day and only planned to stay at Anna's a little while." The words trailed into a sob.

Noah reached for her hand and held it while he digested this new information. The walk from the Lapps' place would take Eva around half an hour, which meant Eva may have gone missing somewhere between nine fifteen and nine thirty. He checked the time on his phone. More than three hours had passed. Finding Eva quickly was imperative. The first forty-eight hours were critical in a missing persons case.

An ambulance pulled in behind the vehicles, followed

by another police cruiser. Sheriff Walker Collins had arrived on scene.

When the sheriff approached, Noah opened his door. Walker leaned in. "I hear there's been a bit of trouble here tonight?" He introduced himself to Rachel. "EMTs are here. Let's get you looked at."

Getting out, Noah circled around to Rachel's side and opened her door. She stared up at him with a desperate look on her face.

He held out his hand. "Megan and Aden are doing everything they can to find this man. You need to take care of yourself for Eva." He walked her to the ambulance and waited beside her with Walker while EMT Jake Oliver cleaned and bandaged her feet and applied antibiotic cream to the scrapes on her face. Her attacker had slapped her. Why would the man want to hurt someone as sweet as Rachel? Nothing about what happened tonight made sense.

"You'll have some bruising and tenderness for a few days," Jake told her, "but none of your injuries are serious."

A noise behind them sent both Noah and Walker whirling. Aden and Megan headed their way.

"Did you find my sister?" Rachel asked as soon as they were close.

Aden shook his head. "No, I'm sorry, we didn't." He turned to Walker. "The perp parked at the end of the drive. Probably approached without his headlights on to not wake anyone."

Megan handed Rachel a pair of shoes. "I found these by the door and thought they might belong to you."

"Denki," Rachel murmured and slipped her injured feet inside, wincing when she put pressure on them.

"I'll call in the crime scene unit to go over the house

and take photos of the footprints and tire tracks. Hopefully, we can get some answers for you soon," Walker assured Rachel.

She clutched the blanket around her shoulders against the biting wind.

"Let me take you to the house so you can change into something warmer," Noah said, noticing. "Then we'll go to the station. I want you to look through some mug books. You said you ripped the mask off the man?" She nodded. There was a slim chance she might be able to identify the man from the photos. "I know you said you didn't get a good look at him, but maybe going through the books will help you pick him out. While you're doing that, I'll speak to Anna Lapp. It could be that Eva changed her mind and spent the night with her friend and I'll find her there safe and sound."

"I'm going with you," Rachel said without budging. "I want to speak with Anna."

"That's not happening," he assured her without considering it. "Until we're sure what's truly happening here, you need to stay out of sight. Chances are, Eva grew sleepy and decided to spend the night at Anna's house."

"And what if she didn't? What if she is out there somewhere hurt? She could have been in an accident on the way home. I'm going with you to speak with Anna. Eva's my sister, Noah. She needs me." She lifted her chin. The courage he'd seen in her so many times in the past returned.

Noah faced the sheriff. "What do you think?"

Walker considered it for a moment. "The young lady is more likely to answer your questions with Rachel there. Do it," he agreed. "But make sure you check in with Janine when you arrive and before leaving the Lapps' place."

Expelling a breath, Noah accepted Walker's suggestion despite his misgivings. "Okay. But I want you close at all times," he told Rachel. While he understood the benefit of having her at the Lapp interview, he still worried about keeping her safe.

"I've called in Ryan and Cole. I know their shifts don't begin for," Walker glanced at his watch, "another six hours, but we need everyone on this." He surveyed the desolate stretch of road. "We'll set up some floodlights. If she's here, we'll find her."

"What if she's not here?" Rachel's question was directed solely at Noah, and he didn't have an answer.

"The best way you can help Eva now is to identify the man who attacked you."

He noticed her shivering still and took off his coat and placed it over her shoulders. "It's freezing out. Let's get you inside the cruiser where it's warm."

He and Rachel headed toward his SUV along with Walker. Rachel braced against the biting wind that threatened to knock her down. The Montana weather could be brutal, and it appeared winter was setting in early in the shadow of the mountains. Though barely November, already they'd had several feet of snow.

He clutched her arm to keep her steady. Opening the door, he waited until she slid inside.

"Looks like the rest of the team is here." Walker crooked a thumb behind them.

Noah mentioned the Beacheys coming to investigate. "It's possible they saw the man."

"I'll have someone speak to them. We'll start canvassing every square inch of the place," Walker said. "I'll let you know the minute we have anything."

"Thanks." Noah asked Megan to ride over with them to the house so she could stand guard while Rachel changed.

While Megan hopped in the back, Noah got in next to

Rachel. She appeared in a daze. Noah prayed they would find Eva alive.

He touched her arm. "Don't give up hope." She twisted in her seat. The desperation on her face made him want to gather her close. He didn't have that right anymore. He'd broken her heart once, and he doubted she'd want his comfort now. Instead, he put the SUV in Drive and slowly turned around and eased past the slew of police vehicles.

Driving the short distance to her house, Noah parked out front. He couldn't imagine how terrified Rachel had been to awaken and find a masked stranger standing over her.

The three of them got out and went inside.

"Here, put these on," Megan said and handed Rachel a pair of latex gloves. "We don't want to contaminate any evidence the attacker may have left behind."

Rachel slowly nodded and took the gloves.

"I'll be right out here," Noah assured her when she hesitated.

The bedroom door closed behind them, and quiet returned to the house. Taking out his flashlight, he shined the light around the living room he remembered from his youth. The furnishings appeared the same. A couple of rockers flanked the woodstove, a sofa across from them. A small wooden desk placed under the window. He pictured Rachel sitting there, looking out at the breathtaking views of the mountains she loved so much with that awestruck gleam in her eyes that he remembered from the past. As kids, they used to play all over these mountains. Knew every square inch by heart.

Seeing her home again flooded his heart with bittersweet memories. Rachel's family had treated him like one of their own. His childhood home was a stone's throw from theirs, at the edge of the West Kootenai Amish Community. At one time, before that final summer, he'd talked to Rachel about joining the Amish faith. When his father found out, he'd become furious. Being Amish was not what his dad had planned for Noah's future. He'd go to college. Make something of himself.

Noah swallowed deep and shoved those images aside. The past was over and done. Nothing he could do would change it now.

He moved to the kitchen dominated by a wood-burning cook stove. To his left, the handmade table Rachel's father, Ezra, created years earlier was covered in a plain white tablecloth, a kerosene lamp sitting in the middle. Two plain wooden benches flanked either side.

A sound close by had him spinning on his heel. Rachel and Megan emerged from the bedroom. The somber black dress Rachel wore was a stark contrast to her white apron and prayer *kapp*. A reminder that she was in mourning. Noah's good friend Isaac Yoder had told him Rachel lost her husband a little more than a year earlier. Another man had loved her. She'd loved him back. That was the hardest part, even though Noah had been the first to marry someone else.

"Ready?" he asked. A tiny frown line appeared between her brows as she watched him. He couldn't imagine the things his expression must be giving away.

Once he'd dropped Megan at the search site, he and Rachel headed for the Lapps' home.

"Do you mind if we go through the events of tonight one more time?" he asked because he needed something to fill the poignant silence hanging between them, and he didn't understand why someone was targeting her and Eva. The Amish were peaceful people.

"I don't mind," she said and smiled at him for the first

time. His chest constricted at the sight of it. He remembered the love they'd shared before it had all fallen apart.

"I'd drifted asleep in the chair in my bedroom while reading," she said, her voice but a whisper. Noah had no doubt she would have been poring over God's Word, finding comfort there. He'd never understood that need until Olivia's death. Losing his wife had changed things for him.

Even experiencing death firsthand with Olivia, he couldn't begin to understand how difficult the past four years had been for Rachel. Isaac told him about her father dying after he'd suffered a heart attack working in the field. If that wasn't bad enough, her husband passed last year in a buggy accident…and now this.

"I wanted to wait up for Eva, but I grew sleepy." Her voice trailed off. Was she reliving the nightmare? "Noah, I couldn't breathe. He held his hand over my mouth and nose. I thought he would kill me."

Noah had interviewed countless victims during his time on the force. He understood how difficult recounting the details of an attack could be. But Rachel wasn't just any victim. He had a personal connection with her. Seeing her again made him feel like that young boy who had been crazy about her and desperate to find a way to defy his father and make her his.

"What happened next?" he gently asked when she grew quiet.

"He forced me out of the chair and tried to make me go with him." She stopped for a breath. "Then he said, 'He has plans for you.'"

His brows slanted together after hearing this again. "Have you figured out what he might have meant by that?"

Her beautiful gaze locked to his as realization dawned

on her face. "Oh, no," she whispered, her hand covering her mouth.

"What is it?" He dreaded her answer.

"I just remembered something that happened a few days ago when I was coming home from work at Christner's Bulk Foods Store… I help Esther Christner out a couple of days a week," she explained. "Noah, I think someone followed me from the town. When I was on my way home, a car sped past me and stopped suddenly halfway on the road. At the time, I thought the driver might have car trouble. But now, after what happened tonight…if another vehicle had not come along…" Her voice trailed off.

Noah's gut told him the driver of the car had planned to take her then. The second vehicle had foiled the attack. Someone was deliberately coming after Rachel, and he needed to find out who before it was too late. For Eva. For Rachel.

TWO

Eva, where are you? Rachel felt so helpless. All she could think about was what might be happening to her sister.

Shutting out the dreadful thoughts was hard, but she had to keep it together for Eva.

She shifted in her seat. "Do you remember the Lapps live up this road on the right?" As much as she hoped they'd find Eva fast asleep at Anna's home, she did not expect it.

"I do," Noah said and glanced her way. "Until we catch this guy, the less you're out in public, the better. The safest place for you now is at the station."

He was worried about her. She understood, but she had to do whatever she could to find her sister because the thought of losing Eva was unbearable.

"I'm safe with you," she said. "And Anna might tell me something she would be too nervous to say with just you alone."

Holding her gaze a long moment, he sighed and tapped the radio on his jacket. "Janine, I'm making a stop at the Lapp place on Spruce before heading to the station. I have Rachel Albrecht with me. Walker knows, but I wanted you to be aware, as well. I'll radio you when we're heading your way."

"Copy that," the dispatcher said.

While Noah concentrated on his driving, Rachel tried

to imagine him as a deputy sheriff. He'd loved working on his family's farm and helping her *daed* out whenever possible. She'd always assumed he'd one day own his own farm, yet something had changed him.

Seeing him again after all these years felt unreal. When she'd first learned that his family had moved from the area, she'd been devastated. There had been no goodbye—no explanation. Her *mamm* was the one to break the news to her. All along, she'd known his family didn't approve of their relationship, but she'd thought he would stand up for her. For them.

Back then, her whole world revolved around the time they spent together. Even though Noah wasn't Amish, her young heart believed they could find a way to work through all the problems facing them as long as they had each other.

He caught her looking at him and she dropped her gaze to her hands. Her palms stung from the cuts there. The worry for Eva threatened to swallow her up. She was barely hanging on.

Noah turned off Spruce and eased the patrol vehicle down the potholed dirt road leading to the Lapps' home. Once they reached it, he killed the engine. The house was dark inside. The family of six would be sleeping. Morning came early in Amish country. As dairy farmers, the Lapp men would be up before dawn to start the morning chores.

"We're going to have to wake them. There's no other choice." He focused on his watch. "It's almost two." With a sigh, he glanced her way. "This won't be easy." Climbing out, Noah came around to her side. He'd grown up a lot over the years. Still, no matter how much he'd changed, when she looked at him, she saw the young boy she'd once adored.

Slightly taller now, he'd filled out from that lanky teen,

but those brilliant blue eyes were much the same, as was the blond hair, though he'd cut it much shorter now. She'd thought about him a lot over the years. Wondered. Kept the pain to herself. Her *mamm* had been the only one who knew how broken Rachel was after Noah left.

"Ready?" he asked when she stood beside him.

Letting go of the past was hard. Her life had been blessed. She and Daniel had many happy years together. And a life spent lingering on regrets is a wasted life, her *mamm* always said.

She nodded, the hurt too fresh to trust her voice.

Noah stepped up on the porch with her. It took several knocks before someone rousted. Samuel Lapp opened the door a crack, holding a lantern high, concern etched across his face.

"Mr. Lapp, I'm sorry to wake you so early. I'm Deputy Noah Warren, and you know Rachel Albrecht. We need to speak with your daughter Anna immediately."

Samuel's gaze shot to Rachel. She couldn't imagine how pitiful she must look.

"What is this about, Deputy?" Samuel asked.

"It's about Eva, sir. She didn't come home last night. Is she here?"

Samuel's eyes widened and he shook his head. "*Nay.* Eva left hours ago." The worst possible news. Rachel struggled to hold herself together.

"We believe your daughter may have been the last person to see her," Noah said. "That's why we need to speak with her."

Samuel gasped, his bushy white brows shooting up. "What could have happened to Eva? This is a peaceful community. There's been no crime."

Noah glanced at Rachel. "We're not sure. We're hoping Anna can shed some light."

"*Jah*, please come inside." Samuel held the door open, and they stepped across the threshold. His wife, Kathryn, stood beside her husband.

"What has happened to Eva?" Kathryn asked with a fearful expression on her face. Rachel could not speak the darkest fears of her heart aloud.

"She didn't come home last night. We don't know where she is," Noah answered for her.

"Go quickly," Samuel said, facing his wife. "Wake Anna."

With a worried glance at Rachel, Kathryn hurried away. In the awkward silence that followed, Rachel's concern for Eva's safety continued to grow.

Noises above were followed by voices. Anna came swiftly down the stairs with Kathryn at her heels.

"Anna, Eva did not come home last night. What time did she leave here?" Samuel asked his daughter.

Anna's eyes widened. "I'm not sure. She wanted to be home by ten, and it's a good walk to her house. She left in plenty of time, though. I cannot believe she didn't make it home."

"Did she mention if anything was bothering her lately?" Noah asked. "Was she having a problem with anyone? A boy, perhaps?"

Anna's troubled gaze shot to Rachel. "She was happy. She talked to a lot of different people at the singing, but there was no special boy. She was so excited about taking over the teaching position soon. We had fun at the singing. When it ended, we came home. I made cocoa, and we talked for a while." Anna smiled at the memory. "Eva spoke of the lessons she and Hannah planned for the *kinner* the next day and asked if I wanted to stop by sometime and sit in on the class. Eva knows I want to become a teacher, too, and thought it might be helpful. Once she takes over the position, she plans to speak to the community elders about letting me apprentice." Tears shone in Anna's eyes. "Eva was happy and excited about her work. There was nothing wrong."

"Did anyone pay special attention to her at the social?" While Rachel understood Noah had to ask the question, she couldn't envision anyone from the community wishing Eva harm.

"No, no one."

Noah barely hid his disappointment. "We appreciate your help, Anna. I'm sorry to wake you and your family so early. If you remember anything else, please let me know."

He started to leave, but Anna grasped his arm. "You have to find her, Deputy. Please, she's my best friend." Kathryn placed her arms around her weeping daughter's waist and drew her close.

"We're going to do our best to bring her home safely," Noah assured her.

Samuel stepped out on the porch with them. "If we can help in any way, please let us know. Eva is like one of our own," he told Rachel.

"*Denki*, Samuel," Rachel managed through tears. She turned away, trying to hold on for Eva's sake.

"Do you think it's possible you or Anna wouldn't know if Eva was seeing someone?" Noah asked when they were inside the SUV again.

Rachel couldn't imagine Eva keeping something like that secret. "It's not possible. Eva and I are close. She tells me everything that is happening in her life. She would not keep something like that to herself."

The doubt she saw in him hurt. "It wouldn't be the first time something like this happened. Teenagers keep secrets. It's part of the age."

"Perhaps in the *Englisch* world, but not here amongst the Amish. Eva would not lie to me."

Without answering, Noah reversed the SUV, spun around and headed down the long drive. Hitting the radio on his shoulder, he spoke to the dispatcher again. "Show us leaving the Lapps' place, Janine. We're heading your way."

"Will do. See you soon."

Once he reached the end of the drive, he stopped. "You said you think someone was following you. Did anything else happen before the incident the other day? What about with Eva? Did she mention anything strange going on?"

"No, nothing. And Eva never said a word about anything out of the ordinary happening."

He pulled onto Spruce once more and headed toward Eagle's Nest. "By the way, where is Beth?"

Rachel leaned against the headrest as exhaustion settled in her limbs. "*Mamm* left last week to visit her sister and parents in Colorado. *Aenti* Deborah has not been feeling well for a while. *Mamm* wanted to spend some time with her to help nurse her to good health."

Noah smiled over at her, gentleness in his eyes. "I was sorry to hear about your father. He was a good man."

She ducked her head. "*Jah*, he was." Even though four years had passed since her *daed* died, at times, she still couldn't believe he was gone.

Her *mamm* had become worried about him when he didn't show up for the evening meal. She'd asked Rachel's husband to check on him, and Daniel had found *Daed* passed out in the field he'd been working. He'd suffered a heart attack. Her *daed* never recovered.

Shaking off those sad memories, she tried to focus on Noah's earlier question. Other than the incident with the car, she had no proof anyone was watching her, only a feeling.

A frown creased Noah's handsome face. He watched something in the rearview mirror.

She glanced behind them. Headlights. "Is something wrong?"

"I'm not sure. That car came out of nowhere the moment we left the Lapps' drive. I think they were waiting for us."

Fear gathered her in its embrace. Someone was following them.

The vehicle came closer. Noah's bad feeling doubled. The headlights were on bright. What was the driver trying to do? Noah slowed the SUV's speed, thinking if the incident was innocent, the driver would pass them. Did they not know they were tailgating a sheriff's deputy?

As he continued to watch his rearview mirror, he noticed something alarming. The car's front license plate was missing. With the vehicle inches from his bumper, Noah prepared to radio for assistance, when the car rammed the rear of the patrol vehicle.

Noah lurched forward, the seat belt caught hard. Out of the corner of his eye, he noticed Rachel gripping the armrest for support.

The SUV slipped on the icy road and he struggled to keep it under control.

"What's happening?" she asked, her voice unsteady and barely audible.

"They're trying to run us off the road." The car edged up behind them once more. Noah floored the gas pedal. The SUV fishtailed, and he held on to the wheel with all his might to keep from losing control. The car stayed with him.

"Hold on," Noah yelled when the car slammed into them again. Before he had time to radio for assistance, the rear tire of the SUV blew. The vehicle spun three hundred and sixty degrees on the ice before heading straight for the snow-covered ditch at full speed.

Noah fought for control and lost. The cruiser hit the snow hard, launched itself through the air and slammed onto its side. Skidding some twenty feet, it plowed up snow and debris until it came to a shuddering stop on the passenger side. His head slammed against the driver's-side window. It shattered on contact, sending glass flying everywhere. Noah lost consciousness briefly. When he came to, seconds ticked away before the fog lifted. Blood oozed from his face where bits of glass embedded.

Rachel! Below him, a barely audible moan. He glanced down to see her suspended by the seat belt. "Rachel, are you hurt?" Her lack of response was terrifying. Noah craned his neck. The dashboard lights revealed her eyes were not open. She wasn't moving.

"Rachel!" he called to her again. Her eyes fluttered open. Breath seeped out in a sigh of relief. Still, she could have internal injuries. "Are you okay? Can you move?" he asked.

She flexed her arms and legs. "I think so."

A flashlight's beam swept across the windshield. Rachel's eyes shot to Noah's. He signaled for her to keep silent. The men who ran them off the road were still out there.

Noah's radio hung freely from his jacket, smashed to bits when he'd slammed into the door. He couldn't find the cell phone that he'd placed on the center console. They were on their own.

"See if you can unfasten your seat belt," he whispered with urgency.

It took several tries before she was free.

"Stay down and don't move no matter what," he said in a low voice. Rachel flattened herself against the floorboard.

It took all his effort to unholster his Glock.

"Be careful, he's a cop," a man's voice warned. He had to be standing right next to the SUV.

"Yeah, well, you'd better hope she's alive because he's going to be angry if you killed her by ramming their vehicle. We were supposed to follow them. Find out what's going on. See if we could get her alone and nab her, and now you've gone and done this."

"Shut up. I got the job done, didn't I? We have them at our mercy," the first man snapped.

"By running a sheriff's vehicle off the road! You could land us both in jail. I want my share of the money. If she's dead or we get caught, there's nothing."

"She's not dead, and there's no way I'm going to jail, not even if I have to kill him." Rachel's terrified gaze met his. "Besides, they're probably both unconscious. And we're wearing masks. Now, give me a foot up so I can grab her before he wakes up."

Outside his door, Noah heard the men struggling to reach it. A man's head and shoulders popped into view. In the cramped position, Noah aimed and fired. The man yelped and fell backward.

"I'm hit," he screamed. "He shot me. Help me out, why don't you. We need to split. There could be more of them coming."

"What about the girl? We need her," his partner said.

"Forget the girl. We'll get her another time," the first man snapped. "I've been shot! I need a doctor."

Seconds slipped by. A car's engine fired. Tires squealed as the vehicle sped away.

"Let's get out of here before the one guy changes his mind and decides he'd rather have the money than save his buddy's life." Noah tried to free the latch on the seat belt, but the tension of his weight against it was too much.

He felt around on the center console, unable to open it from his angle.

"I'm going to need your help. I have a knife in the center console. Can you reach it?"

Using the seat as a crutch, Rachel managed to stand. Opening the console, she felt around until she located the knife.

"I have it." She held it up.

He took it from her. "Once I cut through the seat belt, I'm not sure if I can control where I'll land, and I'm afraid I'll hurt you in the process. Can you make it to the back seat? You should be safe there."

She glanced behind him. "I think so." Gathering her skirt, Rachel eased between the two seats until she was tucked behind the passenger seat.

Noah braced his weight against the console. Opening the knife, he began cutting away at his restraints.

It took longer than he'd expected for the final piece to fray loose and free him. His full weight slammed against the console, which blocked his fall. Wincing in pain, he breathed a prayer of thanks. He spotted his cell phone where it had landed in the passenger side pouch. Grabbing it, Noah quickly called Walker.

"Where are you? Janine said you were heading to the station a while ago."

Drawing in a breath, Noah explained about the attack. "The SUV's incapacitated and I'm afraid those goons might return to try and kidnap Rachel again."

"We're on our way. Can you two make it out of the cruiser?"

"I think so."

"Good. Find someplace safe to hide until we arrive. We're ten minutes out." Sirens blared through the phone.

Ending the call, Noah pocketed the phone. He killed the SUV's engine and peered out the shattered driver window.

"I think we can climb out this side and then scoot across to the front of the SUV and hop to the ground." Noah eased out the window and moved a little away. He held out his hand to her.

Bracing her foot, Rachel grasped it, and he lifted her up and out of the patrol vehicle. She glanced over the side. It was a good drop straight down.

"Don't look down, just do what I do, okay?" He held her gaze. Slowly she nodded. On his hands and knees, Noah edged to the front of the vehicle. As carefully as possible, he put one foot on the headlight and the second on the grill. He jumped down, the deep snow cushioned his landing.

Holding out his hands, he looked up at Rachel, reading all her doubts in her eyes. "It's okay. I have you. I'm not going to let you fall." He'd let her down once. Would she trust him this time?

"You promise?" she asked, her voice filled with uncertainty.

"I promise. I won't let you down again." And he meant it. No matter what, he'd do his best to keep her safe and bring Eva home to her family.

With the tiniest of nods, she placed her feet where he had. His hands circled her waist, and he lowered her to the ground at his side still holding her close. Their gazes tangled. All her doubts there for him to see. The past enveloped him once more, as did his regret.

Pushing against his hands, she stepped back, and he felt her rejection almost like a blow.

Noah cleared his throat. "We'd better get out of sight until Walker arrives." Taking her hand, he headed up the snowbank to the woods close by, while his thoughts ground out all sorts of possibilities. *I want my share of the money. If she's dead, we get nothing.* The brazen attack on a law enforcement officer along with the unveiled threat to kill Noah if necessary proved these men would stop at nothing to get to Rachel. And if what happened here tonight was any indication, Noah wasn't so sure he could protect her if they did.

THREE

She squeezed her eyes shut. The fluorescent lights bored into her head. It throbbed with pain. All she could think about was Eva. What Anna said confirmed the truth in her mind. Eva never made it home. Someone kidnapped her like they'd tried to do to Rachel. What did these men want with them?

So far, after looking at dozens of photos of criminals for hours, the man who attacked her wasn't among them—at least as far as she could tell. All she had to go on was his eyes, but they left a lasting impression.

Noah promised to find Eva. As the hours slipped away, she struggled to hold on to that promise.

Holy Father in Heaven, please bring my schweschder *home safely.*

She'd lost so much in her life. Noah. Her *daed*. Daniel. The baby. At times, it felt as if the pain in her heart would be there to stay. She couldn't lose her sister, too.

Against her will, she remembered that fateful day. She and Daniel were heading home from the bulk foods store. To this day, she still didn't know what spooked the mare. Daniel was thrown. He'd died before he reached the hospital. When her doctor visited her some time later, he delivered another blow. Losing their unborn baby was just the beginning. He'd told her the damage to her body was too great. She would not likely be able to have another child.

Something brushed against her hand. Rachel's eyes snapped open. A Styrofoam coffee cup sat next to her. She glanced up. Noah was there.

"I thought you could use a break." He smiled, and she noticed his facial cuts from the glass had been bandaged. He pulled out the chair next to hers.

"Denki," she murmured and took a sip. Strong coffee. Something she rarely drank anymore. Daniel was the coffee drinker in the family. Since his passing, she couldn't bring herself to prepare it for herself.

"How are you holding up?" he asked, keeping a careful watch on her face.

Truthfully, she was barely hanging on. "I feel so helpless. I need to be doing something. I can't sit here looking at these photos any longer while Eva is missing." She shook her head. "She could be hurt, Noah. Maybe a car struck her on the way home, and she's lying out there frightened and alone. I am supposed to watch out for her. My *mamm* entrusted her well-being to me." Not since losing Daniel had she felt such turmoil in her heart.

Noah covered her hand with his. "We have all our people looking for her. They're combing the road between the Lapp place and yours. We'll find her." His gentle answer washed over her, and she pulled in a breath. Gazing into his eyes, she believed him. Noah was a *gut* man. He would do what he could to fulfill his promise and bring Eva home.

As she studied his handsome face, the past and all its shattered dreams rose in her heart like a barrier between them. At seventeen, she had been so sure her future belonged with Noah. It didn't matter how many times her *mamm* tried to get her to see the differences standing between them. She'd been so foolish back then, blinded to the truth while her heart had believed that with Noah at her side they could conquer any obstacle in their way, including their differences in faith.

But the past had no place between them anymore.

She studied his handsome face. While his blue eyes were as she remembered, fine lines fanned out around them. Grooves circled his mouth. She wondered about his life now. Was he married? Happy?

"I've been so worried about Eva that I haven't thought to ask how you've been."

Dark blond brows shot up. Time slipped by before he answered. "I've been okay, I guess. Busy. This job is fulfilling in many ways." A strange answer. He stopped, and she wondered if perhaps in just as many ways it was not.

"I meant what I said earlier. I am sorry about Ezra. He was like a dad to me for a long time. I learned a lot about farming from Ezra when I was too stubborn to listen to my father." A hint of a smile lifted the corners of his mouth, not reaching his eyes. "And I was sorry to hear about your husband, as well," he added quietly.

The strain between them now was something the younger Rachel could not have imagined. They were like two strangers. She glanced at his hand on hers. He didn't wear a wedding band. Had he ever married?

Rachel thought about her years with Daniel. At times, it was hard to believe he was gone. So many things changed forever with his death. The buggy accident that took his life scarred her deeply and she still struggled to accept Daniel's death and her injuries as part of *Gott*'s plan. The future and its promises had evaporated that day.

When the silence between them grew uncomfortable, she asked the question she was curious about. "How did you know about Daniel?"

"Isaac. We still keep in touch. He and I go hunting together several times a year, and I help him with his planting like I used to with your dad."

She looked away, surprised by the admission. When he'd left, Rachel had thought Noah had shut both her and the Amish ways out of his life, and yet he kept in touch with Isaac. He just hadn't wanted her.

Before she could think of anything to say, someone came into the room. The sheriff motioned to Noah. From his grim expression, she was sure something terrible had happened.

Noah stepped out of the room. Her heart accelerated. *Please,* Gott, *do not let it be Eva.*

Time seemed to stop while her last conversation with Eva came to mind.

Can you believe it, Rachel? Soon, I will be teaching at the same shool *where you and I attended as* kinner. *I cannot imagine doing anything else.* Eva's eyes lit up every time she spoke about the future.

Perhaps someday you will meet a man like Hannah Wagler did and fall in love, Rachel had teased.

Her sister had blushed and eventually giggled before changing the subject. At the time, Rachel hadn't thought much about it. Now she wondered if perhaps Eva had kept parts of her life secret even from Rachel.

When Hannah first came to Eva and mentioned her plans to marry Isaac Yoder, the bishop's *sohn*, come November, Eva could not believe that the community leaders would select her to train as Hannah's replacement.

Her sister pored through all of Hannah's past issues of the *Blackboard Bulletin*, an Amish teachers' magazine. Eva could not wait to complete her apprenticeship.

Noah came back in. The sight of him had her jumping to her feet. "Is there news?" she asked while trying to glean something from his expression.

He hurried to her side. "We haven't located her," he said as if reading her thoughts.

"But you know something." She could see it in his eyes.

"Yes, we found this." He held up something in a plastic bag. Rachel's hand covered her mouth. It was Eva's quilted bag. She had had it with her at the church service.

"You recognize it," Noah confirmed.

She nodded. "It belongs to Eva. I made it for her seventeenth birthday six months ago. She took it with her wherever she went. Where did you find it?"

"Not far from where the men forced us off the road." He paused a moment. "Rachel, it's looking more like the man who attacked you and ran us off the road took Eva against her will. I'm guessing they were waiting for her when she left the Lapps' place, much like they were for us."

Rachel sank back into the chair, covering her face with hands that shook. She should have insisted on picking her sister up at Anna's. Eva had assured her everything would be fine, and Rachel was trying to give her sister more freedom, but she'd had doubts. Why hadn't she listened to them?

"This isn't your fault. You can't blame yourself. These guys are ruthless."

Tears filled her eyes. "Isn't it? I should not have let her walk home alone. It was dark and cold. This is my fault."

Noah clasped her hand once more. "Eva is growing up. She's not that little girl who used to tag along all the time."

He was right. Eva was scheduled to join the church in a few weeks' time.

"What do we do now?" she asked because she had to do something to help.

"If you feel up to it, we could go to your place and take a look around. See if anything is missing. The crime scene unit finished a few hours ago. They didn't find anything useful, I'm afraid, although we weren't expecting any fingerprints since you said the man who attacked you wore gloves."

Rachel rose. "*Jah*, I'm ready. I want to do something for Eva."

Noah smiled at her. "Good. I'll let Walker know, and then I'll come get you."

Alone again, the plastic container holding Eva's bag called out to her. She couldn't take her eyes off it. Picking it up, Rachel examined the bag she'd lovingly quilted for her sister. Specks of dark red covered the broken shoulder strap. Blood.

The plastic bag slipped from her fingers. Drawing in a breath, she struggled to keep from being sick.

"What happened to you, Eva?" she whispered while all sorts of possibilities, none of which were good, raced through her head.

She closed her eyes. Nothing made sense. Someone had kidnapped Eva and tried to do the same to her. What could they possibly want?

The door opened. Rachel spun away and tried to reclaim her composure.

"What's wrong?" Noah asked from near the door.

Squaring her shoulders, she faced him. She had to stay strong. "Nothing. I'm *oke*."

He came to where she stood. "We don't know anything for sure."

She managed a nod and Noah pressed her hand before releasing it.

"We're all set with the sheriff. Let's get out of here." He held the door open for her.

Noah stopped at the front desk where a woman around

the same age as Rachel's *mamm* answered phones. She'd been introduced to the woman earlier.

"Janine, we're heading out to Rachel's house to take a look around. If you need me, you can reach me on the radio."

"Okay, Noah. I'll let Stephanie know, as well. She'll be starting her dispatcher shift in a few hours." Janine smiled sympathetically at Rachel. "It was nice to meet you. I'll say a prayer for your sister."

Touched by the woman's kindness, Rachel waved and followed Noah out into the dawning of a new day filled with threatening gray clouds. At this time of the year, the weather could turn from pleasant to winter cold without a moment's notice.

Noah unlocked a new patrol car and caught her staring at it. "It's the backup unit. It looks like mine is going to be out of commission for a while." He opened the door for her, and she climbed inside.

Driving to the farm, Rachel couldn't keep from glancing over her shoulder, expecting the men who ran them off the road to reappear. Her nerves were all but shattered.

"No one's back there," Noah said quietly, and she shifted in her seat to face him.

"I know," she said but still couldn't relax. Her sister's welfare was foremost in her mind. The last time she'd seen Eva, she was excited about attending the youth group singing. Now Eva was missing. Would she ever see her sister again?

"How are your grandparents?" Noah asked, drawing her attention from her worried thoughts. Growing up close to her family, Noah knew her grandparents well.

"They are *gut*. They moved to the San Luis Valley community in Colorado several years back to live with

Aenti Deborah. They said they couldn't handle the Montana winters any longer."

Her *grossdaddi* suffered from severe arthritis, and the cold became harder to endure with each passing year. He and *Grossmammi* moved to San Luis Valley because of its lower altitude.

Rachel thought about what her *mamm*'s reaction would be to learning her youngest daughter was missing.

"How am I going to tell my grandparents and *mamm* about Eva?"

He held her gaze. "Don't get ahead of yourself. We're still trying to piece together what happened to her."

Slowing the car, he pulled onto her drive. As much as Rachel wanted to believe Eva would somehow turn up and this would prove to be some crazy misunderstanding, the little voice in her head assured her nothing could be further from the truth.

She'd lived all her life surrounded by hard work and peaceful family settings. She knew crime existed, but not in her community. At least not until now.

"You must miss Beth a lot." He glanced her way curiously.

She swallowed deep. "I do." The past year without Daniel had been a difficult one. Losing the baby. The news she would probably never be able to carry another child again threatened to destroy her. She'd relied on Beth's strength to get through the long days. Her *mamm* understood Rachel's crippling grief all too well.

"I'm sure it must have been hard on her to lose Ezra like she did," Noah said. His cell phone rang before Rachel could answer. He spoke briefly to someone before ending the call.

"That was Walker. They found the vehicle that ran us

off the road abandoned off Highway 37. It had been wiped clean, but there was some blood on the passenger seat."

Her heart raced. There was blood on Eva's bag, as well.

"It's probably from the man I shot." Noah's calm voice interrupted her dark thoughts. "A shoulder wound could result in a lot of blood loss."

Still, doubts crawled in. What was happening to her peaceful world? Why was someone trying to hurt her family?

Noah stopped in front of the house, and Rachel stared up at it. She'd lived here all her life. When she and Daniel wed, they moved in with her parents. Her *mamm* and *daed* took over the *dawdi haus* where her grandparents had lived before they moved to Colorado. These walls captured so many good memories, yet what stood out in her mind the most was what happened last night. She could almost feel the man's hand covering her mouth once more, the hatred in his eyes. The last breaths leaving her body. Would she ever be able to get those horrific memories out of her head and feel safe here again?

She noticed something that sent a chill down her spine. The front door stood wide open. An accident? Or had her attacker come looking for her once more?

Noah was on alert the second he spotted the open door. "Wait here and lock the door behind me." He drew his weapon and climbed out of the vehicle. The locks snapped into place. He moved toward the opening.

Had one of the officers from crime scene left the door open? The men and women in that unit were professionals. They wouldn't have acted so carelessly.

Doubts wouldn't go away as he slipped inside the house. What he saw there made it clear this was no accident.

Someone had tossed the place. Furniture was turned over. Chair cushions ripped open. Drawers emptied in a quest to locate something.

He stopped to listen. A noise of something being knocked over came from the *dawdi haus*. Someone was here.

Noah didn't dare call for backup for fear of alerting the intruder. Slowly, he moved down the hall to the *dawdi haus* entrance. As he stood outside the door, not a sound came from inside. Easing the door open, the room in front of him appeared empty. The side door leading outside was cracked.

Rachel!

The noise of glass breaking sent him running through the house. He stepped out onto the porch. What he saw there scared the daylights out of him.

The patrol's passenger window was broken. An armed man with his face obscured by a ski mask held Rachel close. A gun pointed at her head.

Noah reacted immediately. "Drop the gun. Now!" His eyes held Rachel's. "Everything is going to be okay," he tried to assure her.

The man shook his head. "She's coming with me, Deputy. We need her."

The man's words mimicked what the others had said. What were these men after?

"You're not going anywhere. Drop the weapon." Noah kept his aim on the man's head, the only clear shot he had.

The gunman grew increasingly nervous. He glanced down the drive. Was he alone or…? The thought barely cleared Noah's head before a car's engine roared to life. Tires squealed. The man's partner had deserted him.

"Looks like you're all alone. Drop the weapon now," Noah ordered once more.

The man hesitated. His eyes darted from Rachel to Noah's Glock. Without warning, he shoved Rachel away and opened fire. Rachel hit the ground, putting her hands over her head while Noah ducked behind the cruiser as bullets tinged off its side.

Silence followed. He peeked around the side of the vehicle. The shooter was getting away.

Noah ran after him. "Stop right there!" The man kept moving. Noah aimed for his leg and fired. With a blood-curdling yelp, the man grabbed his leg and stumbled to the ground. The weapon flew from his hand and landed some distance away.

Securing the weapon behind his back, Noah kept the Glock trained on the man as he advanced.

"You shot me," the man said in disbelief while holding his leg. Noah rolled him onto his stomach and secured his hands. A search of his pockets produced nothing of any use.

He radioed for help. "Janine, I need immediate assistance." Noah briefly explained what took place.

"Are you both all right?" Janine asked in amazement.

"We're fine, but we'll need an ambulance. The perp's been shot."

Hauling the man up on his good leg, Noah helped him over to the porch where Rachel waited.

"Ouch. Are you trying to kill me? I've been shot."

"Keep quiet," he told the man. Noah turned to Rachel. "Are you okay?"

She managed to nod.

Taking off his belt, Noah secured it above the gunshot wound to slow the blood flow before removing the ski mask. He didn't recognize the man. His voice wasn't familiar, either. He wasn't one of the two who ran them off the road. How did he fit into what was happening?

"Do you know him?" he asked Rachel, but could tell from her reaction she didn't.

"What's your name?" Noah asked.

The man glared at him. "Lawyer. I want a lawyer." Without another word, he clamped his mouth shut. There would be no answers coming from this man.

Within minutes, two cruisers pulled onto the lane followed by an ambulance.

After exiting from their vehicles, Deputies Ryan Sinclair and Cole Underwood, along with Sheriff Collins, walked purposefully to Noah.

"When I went inside, the house had been ransacked." Noah explained what happened. Next to him, he heard Rachel's surprise. "I'm sorry." He turned to her. "I'll go with you to make sure nothing is missing." Noah drew in a breath. "I heard glass breaking and ran outside. The man had smashed the passenger window and was holding Rachel at gunpoint." He explained how he'd been forced to shoot the man. "There was someone else here. Whoever it was, he left his partner behind."

"We're ready to take him to the hospital, Sheriff," one of the EMTs said.

Walker nodded. "I'll ride with him. When he's bandaged up, I'll bring him in for questioning. In the meantime, let's get crime scene out here again."

Noah called in the order.

"Cole and I will canvass, see if anything turns up," Ryan said. Noah headed inside with Rachel. He stopped in the doorway and turned to her. "You should prepare yourself. It's pretty messed up."

He stepped across the threshold and waited for her.

She gaped at the wreckage around them. "Why are they doing this? What were they looking for?"

"I don't know," he said gently. "But we'll find out."

Walker came inside and motioned to Noah. "I'm heading out now. I'll leave my cruiser here for you to use. Until we know what we're up against, I want you with Rachel at all times. We'll need to speak with the bishop and clear it with him first. There's an add-on close to the house, correct?"

"Yes. I can bunk down there. I think it would be a good idea to have some of our people stationed outside, as well. Perhaps when Aden and Megan come on duty later today."

"I agree. I'll send them over. Whatever these guys' motives are, they aren't letting up. I'm worried about the sister," Walker said in a low voice for Noah's ears only.

Noah was, too.

"I don't think we'll get anything from this guy until his lawyer arrives. Maybe not even then. If he does decide to talk, I'll let you know. In the meantime, take care of her." Walker nodded to Rachel before leaving.

Noah turned and noticed Rachel kneeling in front of an old quilt chest.

He sensed something was wrong.

"What is it?" he asked.

She clutched a quilt tight. "It's missing." The pain in her eyes was unmistakable. "My *mamm*'s Bible. She kept it in this chest. It belonged to my *grossmammi*. Why would someone want to take the Bible?"

Noah had no answer. What could be so important about a family Bible for someone to tear the place apart to get it? Whatever its connection to the attack and Eva's disappearance, they'd need to figure it out and soon, because he couldn't help but believe time was quickly running out for Eva.

FOUR

"We need to talk to Bishop Aaron and get permission to have deputies stationed in the community as well as at your home," Noah told her. She didn't answer. All she could think about was Eva.

"Rachel, did you hear me?" Noah asked, a worried frown on his face.

Forcing the fear aside, she nodded.

"I'll need you to come with me. Bishop Aaron doesn't exactly have fond memories of me, even though I remain friends with his son."

The truth behind those words slowly dawned and she smiled. Rachel remembered the time Noah spoke of very clearly. Back then, it was her, Isaac and Noah. They'd been inseparable. On one particular day, they'd been picking apples near Isaac's home when Noah decided to toss one like a baseball. Only he'd lost control and sailed it through the Yoders' front window. Bishop Aaron had read them all the riot act. Isaac had been forbidden to play with Noah for a long time. When her *daed* found out, he'd voiced his disappointment in both her and Noah before putting them to work mucking out the barn for two weeks as punishment.

"I think he still remembers your misplaced apple ball." She laughed at the memory and he joined in.

"You are probably right. That's why I need you there. The bishop always thought highly of you."

"I'm happy to help out," she assured him, confident that once the bishop learned what happened to her and Eva, he would agree to allow Noah and his comrades to stay in the community.

"Thanks. Let's see if we can get this mess cleaned up first." He went over to the sofa and muscled it upright before setting the two chairs on their rockers while Rachel tucked the quilts her *grossmammi* had made into her *mamm*'s old chest and went into the kitchen. She began putting away the pots and pans. Noah finished in the living room and helped her out. Once she'd put away the silverware, Rachel picked up the notepad kept in one of the kitchen drawers. The top page had been ripped free. Fear clawed at her insides.

"What's wrong?" Noah asked, catching her expression.

She held up the pad. "I wrote the number to the San Luis Valley General Store down on the pad. *Aenti* Deborah receives calls there. *Mamm* said if I needed to reach her I could use the phone shanty near the shops in West Kootenai to call and leave a message for her." Her gaze held Noah's. "Do you think they will come after my *mamm*?"

His jaw tightened. "I don't know, but I'm going to call the Alamosa County Sheriff's Department near there and alert them to what's happening. Have them keep an eye out on Deborah's house just in case. Until we know for certain your mother is in danger, there's no need to worry her unnecessarily." Noah stepped away to make the call while her focus remained on the imprint of the number left behind on the pad. First Eva, now her. Please, not her *mamm*.

"Ready?" Noah asked. Rachel let go of her fears and followed him to the door. Noah waited while she removed her cloak from the peg and slipped into it, tying her traveling bonnet over her prayer *kapp*.

"I realize it's probably a minimal deterrent, but to be safe, we should lock both doors. Do you have the key to the house?"

Rachel couldn't remember the last time her family locked their doors. West Kootenai was a peaceful community. She never once felt unsafe before.

"I think *Mamm* keeps it in the desk drawer. I'll get it." She opened the drawer and rummaged through the pile of papers there until she found the key. Rachel handed it to Noah.

Together, they stepped out on the porch. Noah locked the front door and slipped the key in his pocket.

The first tiny snowflakes of the day had begun falling from gray cotton clouds.

Noah opened the passenger door for her.

Being near him again brought up a bunch of unresolved feelings she'd held inside through the years. Her chest tightened at the look in his eyes. It reminded her of the sweet boy from her past. The one she'd believed loved her in the same way she did him.

Slipping past him, Rachel sank into the seat, her attention straight ahead. Noah was part of her past. In her heart, she knew she'd never remarry. That part of her life was over. So why was she pining after a boy who had left her behind?

Noah got in next to her. She sensed his eyes on her, but she couldn't think of a word to say. After a minute, he started the car and headed down the drive.

Bishop Aaron's homestead was several miles from hers.

"When was the last time you saw Isaac?" she asked to fill the void between them.

Noah smiled over at her. "Too long. Probably our last hunting trip in January, though he called the station and we talked not too long ago. Isaac's getting married soon. He invited me to the wedding." Noah shook his head. "I can't believe my friend is getting married."

She remembered how close Noah and Isaac were growing up. "I am glad you stay in touch. Hannah is a wonderful young woman. She became the schoolteacher here several years back. I think Isaac was smitten from the moment he met her."

Noah chuckled. "That sounds like him."

"Will you attend the wedding?" The question was out before she could stop it. What had she hoped to gain by asking?

His slanted her a look. "I want to. Do you think it will be a problem with me not being Amish?"

She smiled gently. "You will be welcomed...just maybe not by Bishop Aaron. I am certain he still holds that apple ball against you."

Being with Rachel like this reminded Noah of old times. In the past, they'd spend hours hanging together, taking walks through the woods or exploring the mountains. During her *rumspringa*, when Rachel had more freedom, they'd talk late into the evening. Each time when they had to say goodbye, he hated to let her go. He'd been crazy about her, wanted to spend his life with her—an impossible dream, according to his father. He wasn't part of her world, and she had no place in his. How could they have a future? Even though he'd ultimately agreed with his father, Noah had resented his moving the family away. He'd headed down a self-destructive path.

Getting married at nineteen, Noah knew right away he'd made a colossal mistake. Still, he'd tried to make it work. But between school and work, he and Olivia had rarely seen each other, and when they did, they argued.

Noah spotted the bishop's driveway and turned, letting the past go along with his failures. He alone was responsible for Olivia's death. He'd messed everything up because he'd been angry with his father. A burden Noah would carry the rest of his life and the reason he was determined never to marry again.

As he squinted through the increasingly thick falling snow, the clock on the dash reflected the time. Almost one in the afternoon. More than fifteen hours had passed since they believed Eva had gone missing. Each passing hour meant time was running out for Eva.

He pulled up in front of the house, his gaze going to the window he'd broken as a teen. He recalled how upset Bishop Aaron had been with him.

Rachel's gentle touch on his hand forced his attention to her.

"I don't really think he would hold the apple thing against you after all these years."

The smile on her face took his breath away. He gazed into her beautiful eyes and the past tumbled out as if it were yesterday. He still cared for her. The thought hit him like a lightning bolt.

She ducked her head, breaking the spell.

Clearing his throat, he murmured, "I sure hope not." He climbed out and came around to her side.

Without a word, they stepped up onto the porch, and Noah knocked on the door.

Footsteps slowly advanced through the house, then the door opened. The man standing before them appeared a few years older than Noah remembered, but just as formidable.

"Rachel, *gut* afternoon. I am pleased to see you."

Bishop Aaron smiled. Adjusting his glasses, he took a closer look at Noah. "Noah Warren? Is that you?"

Noah extended his hand. "It's me. How are you, Bishop?"

"Gut, gut." After a moment, he opened the door wide. "Please come inside."

Noah followed Rachel in and closed the door.

The bishop headed toward the kitchen. "May I offer you both some *kaffe?"*

He glanced to Rachel, who nodded. *"Denki,* Bishop. That would be nice."

"I am afraid I'm on my own to make it. Sadie is making her rounds visiting the women in the community. Please sit."

While Noah and Rachel sat on opposite wooden benches flanking the table, the bishop placed coffee into the percolator and added water. He sat the pot on top of the wood cook stove to perk.

"Now, what may I help you with this day?" He glanced over the top of his glasses at them.

Rachel smiled encouragement to Noah.

"Actually, I've come to ask your permission to allow me and several of my deputies to stay on Rachel's property for a bit." Noah filled the bishop in on what had happened.

Shock registered on the older man's face. "I can't believe this is happening here in our community." He faced Rachel. "I'm heartbroken for you and your family. We are a peaceful people, Noah, but under the circumstances…" He stopped, deep in thought for a moment, before nodding. *"Jah,* I will allow it. I think it is a good idea to have your team watching out for Rachel."

Noah was grateful for the man's cooperation. "Thank you, Bishop Aaron."

The bishop inclined his head. "You are welcome. Rachel and her family are very important to our community. You must find Eva and bring her home safely. Whatever I can do to help, I will be happy to."

Bishop Aaron rose to his feet and poured coffee for three, then retrieved cream and sugar.

Noah sipped his. Gaining approval to have a police presence in the community had been a big hurdle, and he was relieved Bishop Aaron gave it so freely.

"I will quietly ask around the community and see if anyone remembers seeing these men. If I find out anything useful, I will be in touch."

Finishing his coffee, Noah said, "I appreciate all your help, Bishop Aaron." He stood along with Rachel. They carried their cups to the sink and washed them out.

"In the meantime, I will let Hannah know what has happened so she won't be expecting Eva at the classroom for a while." Bishop Aaron walked through to the living room and opened the door before facing them again. "I am praying for you both."

The bishop's kindness humbled him. "Thank you," Noah murmured before stepping out into the dreary day.

As he drove back to Rachel's home, Noah's bad feeling assured him they would need God's help more than anything to bring Eva home safely.

Pulling onto the drive, he noted Aden and Megan were in place already. He stopped the car next to them and rolled down the window.

"Things okay here?"

Megan was in the driver's seat. "It's been quiet. We checked around the place when we arrived. There's no sign anyone's been here since the earlier incident."

"Any reports of gunshot victims at the local hospital?" Noah had asked Aden to check with the hospital and clinics around town.

Aden shook his head. "Nothing. Chances are he'd be too afraid of getting caught to go to the hospital."

It made sense.

"We're going to move our patrol car out of sight. We were waiting for you to return first," Megan said.

"Good idea. I'll pull around behind the house," Noah told them. He put the vehicle in gear and waved before they continued.

Parking around back, he and Rachel headed to the front. Reaching the porch, Noah pulled out the key. With Rachel beside him, he unlocked the door and glanced down. What he saw there cemented him in place. A set of muddy footsteps had moved around on the porch. Someone had been there in their absence. Was it Aden and Megan...or the kidnappers? Before he had time to consider the possibilities, a shot ricocheted through the countryside. The bullet whizzed past his head, close enough to feel it move the air.

"Get down," he shouted and grabbed Rachel's hand, tugging her low. Another shot hit the post where he'd stood seconds earlier.

With his breath coming in short bursts, he turned the doorknob and they all but tumbled inside while a barrage of bullets came from the left of the barn. The shooter had waited until he had a clear shot at Noah before opening fire.

Noah slammed the door shut and locked it. The shots had been carefully placed by the sniper to ensure Rachel wasn't harmed. They didn't want her dead, but they were determined to take out any obstacle standing in their way. Namely him.

FIVE

Rachel couldn't stop shaking. Someone had shot at them. In a daze, she watched Noah reach for his cell phone.

"Someone just tried to take me out." He explained what happened to whoever picked up on the other end while Rachel hung on every word. The shooter hadn't been trying to hit her; they'd been aiming for Noah.

"We're both safe. Call me when you know anything." His gaze held hers as he hung up the phone.

"These men definitely want me out of the way so they can get to you." She shivered and he came over to her. "That's not going to happen. Aden and Megan are trying to head the shooter off before he can get away. You're safe, I promise. The house is secure."

She searched his troubled expression. More than anything, she wished she understood what he was thinking.

Noah slowly cleared his throat and stepped back. "It's freezing in here. I'll add some wood to the fire." He moved away and the moment passed.

While he stoked the fire to life, Rachel turned away and placed her hands against her heated cheeks.

She thought she'd dealt with these feelings for Noah. Wrapped them up tight and buried them in a place in her heart she rarely visited anymore. Yet here she was, acting like a young *maede* again. Foolish.

Her life was unraveling. Eva was gone, and Rachel

needed to collect herself. She moved to her bedroom door and stood in front of it. Drawing in a breath, she got the courage to open it and go inside.

Someone had righted the table she'd knocked over while fighting for her life. The kerosene lantern and her Bible sat on top of it. Rachel stared at the rocker where she'd fallen asleep as the horrific images of that night came rushing back. Drawing in a deep breath, she stepped out of the room and closed the door. She'd deal with those memories another day. Instead, she went to her sister's room. Eva kept the space neat and clean. Her *Blackboard Bulletin* magazines were piled on the table next to the bed.

Rachel sank to the bed and picked up the magazines. Flipping through each of them, she remembered how Eva had pored over them for weeks.

A piece of paper slipped out of one of the magazines. Rachel leaned over and picked it up. Her sister had scribbled, "A. Miller. 2 p.m. Stoltzfuses's Bakery." Rachel stared at the paper in shock. She didn't know anyone with the name A. Miller.

Stuffing the paper into the pocket of her apron, she searched the rest of the magazines for more clues. There were none.

A knock on the door sent her jumping to her feet, heart racing. She was on edge, expecting another attack.

Noah stood in the doorway. "Sorry, I didn't mean to spook you." His husky voice dispelled her worries for the moment.

"Is something wrong?" he asked when he saw her expression.

Rachel pulled the slip of paper from her pocket. "I'm not sure. I found this amongst Eva's things." She handed it to him.

"A. Miller." His curious gaze shot to hers. "Do you have any idea who this is?"

She shook her head. "There are no Millers living in the community as far as I know. Eva never mentioned anyone by that name."

He rubbed the back of his neck. "We need to figure out who this person is. I'll call Walker and have him speak with the Stoltzfuses. Perhaps they remember Eva meeting with this man."

"But when? There's no date on the note. Stoltzfuses's Bakery isn't open on Sunday. It could have been last week or longer. Maybe she chose not even to meet this person." She tried not to let the hopelessness inside take control. "You think this is who took her?"

"There's no way of knowing until we talk to this person, but it's something of a lead." He tapped the paper. "I'm going to speak with Sheriff Collins and let him know about this."

Rachel followed him back to the living room. All she could think about was her sister. Why hadn't Eva spoken of meeting this person? She'd believed her sister shared all aspects of her life with her, but now she realized that wasn't the case. What other secrets did Eva keep? All sorts of possibilities sped through her mind, none of them welcome. Had Eva been deceived into a relationship with someone who might end up taking her life?

Noah called Walker and filled him in on the note. "Rachel doesn't recognize the name. As far as she knows there are no Millers living in the community."

"If this guy isn't from around here and he has Eva, who knows where he might have taken her." Walker paused for a breath. "Nothing about this makes sense. If this is all about the younger sister, why come after Rachel unless she saw something and the perps are afraid she can identify them?"

"That could be it," Noah said in a low voice. "The only problem is Rachel doesn't know anything."

Walker's silence didn't sit well. "There is another possibility that we have to consider. Maybe this is connected to the human trafficking ring that's been operating throughout the state. Dozens of young women have disappeared over the years."

Noah didn't want to think about the sweet young girl he'd known going through something so horrific, but the possibility was real enough. Eagle's Nest was but a stone's throw from the Canadian border. If the men managed to get Eva across it...

"Doesn't explain why they'd come after Rachel. They'd want easy targets. She's not an easy target anymore," Noah said and ran a hand across the back of his neck. "Did you get anything from the man I shot?"

Walker's sigh spoke volumes. "Nothing. We printed him. Believe it or not, his prints aren't on file. He claims his name is George Mason and he's a drifter. He's being charged with two counts of attempted murder. The judge denied bail. Maybe sitting in a cell will start him talking."

Noah sure hoped he was right. "That'd be nice. We need some answers."

"Agreed. I don't think he's the mastermind behind all this. He's not that smart. I'm guessing he was sent there to search for something and got caught. Does Rachel have any idea what they might be looking for?"

"None. The Bible that was taken isn't the one used for devotionals."

"We need to figure out what these men want and soon." Walker was silent for a moment. "I'll speak with the Stoltzfuses right away. I know the couple pretty well."

Most of the deputies were familiar with the Amish bakery in Eagle's Nest. The Stoltzfuses were good people. From time to time, Martha dropped off pastries at the station for the officers and just about every deputy on the force stopped by for Martha's apple fry pies.

Noah didn't want to think about what might be happening to Eva. With a heavy heart, he glanced over his shoulder to where Rachel rocked, her attention on the fire. She appeared miles away and deep in thought.

His gaze went to the window. In the distance, the mountains proved a constant reminder that they'd been there long before he arrived and they'd be there long after he was gone.

"As soon as I've spoken with the Stoltzfuses, I'll give you a call." Walker's voice interrupted his musings.

Noah drug his thoughts back to the conversation. "Thanks, Walker." Ending the call, Noah shoved the phone into his pocket.

Doing his best to shake off his concerns, he slipped into the rocker next to Rachel's. "Walker's speaking to the Stoltzfuses," he told her.

She turned in her seat and touched his arm. "*Denki*, Noah. I am grateful you are here with me. I cannot imagine going through this alone."

The sincerity on her face tugged at his heart. "Don't you know I would do anything for you?" he said softly and meant it.

She swallowed visibly. Without answering, she pulled her hand away. "I need to care for the animals. They must be starving by now."

After what had just taken place, Noah wasn't so sure it was safe to leave the house. "First, let me check in with the deputies, then I'll help out."

Aden answered on the first ring. "We're in pursuit of

the vehicle now. I followed them through the woods past the barn. They circled back around to the road. Megan picked me up and we're giving chase. There's no license plate. The car's probably stolen. Hang on a second." The noise of tires screeching resounded through the phone.

"That was close. We almost went off the road. It's pretty icy through here."

"Where are you now?" Noah asked.

"Close to the Lake Koocanusa Bridge."

"Call me as soon as you have them," Noah said and prayed that would happen. "Rachel needs to care for the animals. We'll make it quick."

He ended the call and explained what happened. "We should be okay to do the chores."

Rising, Rachel took her cloak from the peg by the door and slipped into it, then tied her black, deep-set traveling bonnet in place. The dark color of her dress a constant reminder of the man she'd loved and lost.

Noah couldn't picture her with anyone other than him, but what did he expect? That she would wait around for him forever? Besides, he'd married another.

Her sweet voice filtered through his thoughts. He realized she'd been trying to get his attention.

"I'm sorry… What did you say?"

A frown formed between her brows. "Are you okay?"

He nodded and opened the door, relocking it once they were on the porch. Following Rachel to the barn, Noah unlatched the door and stepped inside. Mid-afternoon shadows clung to the corners of the cavernous room.

Taking down the lantern that hung near the door, he struck a match to it. Soft light made the darkness flee.

"I'll muck out the stall and feed the mare for you," he told her, recalling all the times he'd helped with the chores.

She smiled in response and carried the milking stool

over to the cow while Noah cleared up the mare's stall. In the past, he'd enjoyed the hard work, and each minute he'd spent with her had been a blessing.

With the stall clean, he brought over oats and water to the mare, who neighed her appreciation.

Rachel lifted the heavy pail filled with fresh milk and struggled to carry it to the door.

"Here, let me." He took it from her.

"*Denki.* I'll feed the chickens and collect the eggs before we go inside."

Sitting the pail next to the door, Noah glanced around the barn. Not much had changed over the years. A buggy was parked at the far side of the barn away from the animals—the family's means of transportation. Something on the ground next to it seemed out of place, and he went to investigate. Beside one of the wheels, a half-dozen cigarette butts were scattered on the ground. Fire sparked from one of the glowing tips to the hay scattered around on the ground. It caught fire and spread quickly. Noah took off his jacket and began beating out the flames. Rachel rushed over with a bucket of water and tossed it on the flames. The water put out the remaining sparks. With the fire out, smoke billowed from the charred hay.

Noah stomped the remaining butts to make sure they wouldn't ignite. As he surveyed the mess, a chilling thought occurred. What if the butts had been strewn strategically to set a fire and draw one or both of them out of the house in an attempt to separate them and allow the men chasing Rachel to get to her? The shots earlier might be a decoy to get Megan and Aden out of the way.

They'd been gone for almost an hour now. The cigarettes could not have been left by the men they were pursuing. Which meant…someone had been here recently.

SIX

The expression on Noah's face scared her.

"They were just here." Rachel's words slipped out in a whisper.

"There's a chance they could be out there still waiting to ambush us. Go to the back of the barn and get out of sight. Let me check it out."

Before he could move away, she grabbed his arm, keeping him there. She couldn't bear it if something happened to Noah because of her. She couldn't answer the questions in his eyes.

"Please be careful," she murmured.

A breath escaped before he nodded and headed to the door, drawing his weapon in the process. The sight of it brought home the danger facing them.

Noah slipped out of the barn. Rachel moved deeper into its depths, the beat of her heart drowning out all other sounds. Minutes strung together and felt like a lifetime.

A noise near the door had her stepping toward it. Noah. Relief slipped down her limbs. She stopped midstride when a man in a ski mask came inside.

"No." She backed away as he advanced on her. "Noah!" Rachel screamed as loud as she could. Her panicked voice resounded through the barn.

She turned to run. The man grabbed her before she could get away. Rachel screamed and clawed at the hand restraining her, but her efforts were futile. With his arm snaked around her waist, he dragged her along with him while Rachel kicked and screamed again. If he took her, she'd be dead.

The man shoved the door open. Her eyes darted around the area. Where was Noah? Would he reach her in time? As they rounded the corner of the barn, Rachel had to try a last-ditch effort to save her life. She grabbed hold of the side of the barn. The man's hand jerked free. Before he had time to react, she grabbed a shovel leaning against the wall and slugged him hard. He shrieked and staggered backward.

"Rachel! Where are you?" When the man heard Noah's voice, he bolted.

"I'm over here." With her knees threatening to buckle beneath her, she had to keep going. What if the man came back?

Noah appeared in front of her. She all but collapsed into his arms.

"What happened?" he asked.

She couldn't stop shaking as she told him about the man's attempt at kidnapping her.

"Let's get back to the house. There could be others."

With Rachel tucked close to his side, Noah grabbed the pail of milk. She picked up the basket of eggs and they rushed inside and he locked the door.

Noah hit the radio on his shoulder. "Dispatch, I need immediate backup." He told Janine about what happened.

"Megan and Aden are on their way back there now. The car they were chasing got away."

"Unbelievable," Noah murmured.

"I'll dispatch crime scene to your location. Maybe they can get some DNA off the cigarette butts. Walker's en route, as well."

"Thanks, Janine."

With her heart still in her throat, Rachel put away the eggs and milk while trying not to spill either.

Just untying her bonnet proved a near impossible task with hands that shook. Noah saw her distress and helped her out of her cloak. "When was the last time you ate anything?" he asked, the concern on his face clear.

She couldn't remember. Probably at the after-church meal the day before.

"You have to keep up your strength."

The thought of food held no pleasure, but it gave her something to do to keep from going crazy.

In a daze, she went to the kitchen. The clock on the kitchen counter reflected the time. Almost four. Closer to the evening meal than midday. Before what happened last night, her plans for today had been simple.

Yesterday, she'd prepared her sister's favorite meal, scrapple. Taking finely cut pieces of spareribs, she'd boiled them in broth, then added cornmeal until the mixture had a mushy consistency. When it was ready, she'd placed it in the refrigerator to chill overnight. Now she pulled it out and began to heat it in a pan on the stove.

Tears filled her eyes. All she could think about was her sister. *Where are you, Eva?*

Noah came up behind her and gently turned her to face him, spotting her tears.

"Hey, it's going to be okay," he tried to reassure her. "We'll find her." She leaned against him, needing to believe this with all her heart.

Noah enveloped her in his strong arms and held her close. The steady beat of his heart was so familiar. Through the years, Noah had always been her protector. She guessed he still was.

A knock on the door broke them apart. She searched

his face. As a young *maede*, she'd imagined having a family with him, foolishly refusing to see the truth. Their differences in faith were as impossible to summit as the mountains in the distance. There would never be anything between her and Noah. She was not fit to be anyone's wife.

"That's probably Aden and Megan," he assured her and headed to answer the door while she turned back to the stove. Flipping the scrapple before it burned, she tried to calm her frayed nerves.

Both deputies came inside.

"He must have got away on foot before we arrived," Megan said. "Was he alone?"

Noah shook his head, a grim expression on his face. "I don't know. I didn't see any signs there was someone else out there. Crime scene's on the way. Hopefully, they can retrieve some DNA off the cigarettes, but they were pretty badly damaged in the fire."

"Let's hope." Aden didn't sound positive. "We sure could use a break." The deputy's answer did little to settle her fears. Time was ticking away. How much longer did her sweet sister have before it was too late?

Noah recalled the many times he'd shared meals at this same table with Rachel's family, never imagining this day would come.

Several times, he'd noticed Aden watching his and Rachel's interactions curiously. No doubt, witnessing things Noah preferred to keep to himself. He and Aden had been friends since Noah joined the Lincoln County Sheriff's Department. Though Aden knew some of his past—his marriage to Olivia and her death—there was plenty he didn't know. Mostly because talking about Rachel hurt too much.

Once they were all seated at the table, Rachel bowed her head for the silent prayer—a time to quiet one's mind and open the heart up to God. More and more lately, Noah found himself seeking out these moments.

He lowered his head and opened up his heart. *We need Your help, Lord. To find Eva and protect Rachel. To bring these men to justice.*

When he opened his eyes, he found Rachel watching him, a tiny smile on her lips. He wondered if she, too, remembered all the meals they'd shared together.

He hadn't had scrapple since he'd moved away, but hers was just as good as her mother's, though prepared with different hands.

Silence lingered throughout the simple meal. Conversation was hard to come by with so much at stake. Rachel barely touched her food. She scraped back her chair and carried her plate to the sink, her shoulders slumped. Noah couldn't even begin to imagine the fear pressing in on her. Outdoors, red-and-blue lights flashed. The crime scene unit had arrived.

Aden and Megan finished their last bites of food and headed out to assist.

Rachel faced Noah. The despair on her face broke his heart. "You should go," she told him. "They need you. I can take care of the cleanup."

He would give anything to be able to offer her some words of comfort, but he couldn't because he was worried, too. So far, they had nothing.

"It is *oke*," she said with a sad little smile. "I know you are doing everything you can for Eva and me."

He was, but so far it wasn't enough. Though he hated leaving her alone, half the sheriff's department was outside. He doubted the men would try anything. "Make sure you lock both doors behind me."

"I will," she promised without looking at him.

Noah slipped on his jacket and headed out into the cold day. Intermittent snow continued to fall. So far, the accumulation wasn't enough to render the roads hazardous, but it would eventually.

When he entered the barn, Noah noticed Walker by the door talking to Aden.

"Anything?" he asked, stopping next to them.

Walker shook his head. "Nope. The cigarettes are too destroyed for DNA testing. They'll dust the barn for any viable prints.

"How's Rachel holding up?" Walker asked while he watched the crime scene techs work.

"Barely hanging on." Noah wasn't sure how much more she could handle.

"I can imagine. I haven't seen anything like this before."

"Is George Mason talking yet?" Noah asked.

Walker shook his head. "Not a word. I don't think we'll get anything useful out of him. I'd like to speak with Rachel as soon as possible. Maybe now that a little time has passed she'll remember something she didn't think important before."

"Let's hope. She's been through a lot, but she's strong."

Walker spoke to one of the crime scene techs before he and Noah went back to the house and waited for Rachel to unlock the door.

Noah followed Walker inside and closed the door, waiting for his boss to begin.

"Do you mind if we talk for a bit?" Walker asked her.

She glanced from Walker to Noah before shaking her head. "*Nay*, I don't mind. Would you like some coffee?"

Walker smiled at the offer. "That would be nice."

After she poured three coffees, they sat at the table.

Seated next to her, Noah sensed Rachel's uneasiness and reached for her hand.

Walker took a sip before setting down his cup. "Since we don't have any idea what we're up against yet, I want you to think back to a few weeks ago. Can you tell me what happened during that time? Even if it seems insignificant, I want to hear about it."

Noah released her hand and pulled out his pad and pen, ready to write down her answers.

Her brows slanted into a frown. "I'm not sure if this means anything, but two weeks ago my *mamm* left to visit her sister in Colorado. *Aenti* Deborah has been ill for a while with the flu."

"How did she get to Colorado?" Walker prompted.

Rachel stared at him. "She took a bus. I drove the buggy to the bus stop in Eagle's Nest."

Walker nodded. "Did you notice anything unusual while you were in Eagle's Nest? Or on the trip back?"

She thought for a moment. "No, nothing."

Before Walker asked another question, someone knocked on the door.

Noah could feel Rachel's startled reaction from where he sat.

"Let me answer it," he told her and moved to the door. Pulling it open, he was surprised to see Anna Lapp standing on the porch.

"Is Rachel here?" she asked in a tentative voice.

"She is. Come inside, Anna." Noah stepped aside and let the young woman pass.

Anna's gaze darted around the room.

"Is something wrong?" Rachel asked and hurried to Anna's side.

The young woman appeared as pale as a sheet. "I need to speak with you about something important."

"What is it?" Rachel asked.

Anna glanced at the two men before answering. There were tears in her eyes. "I didn't tell you the truth when you asked me about Eva before."

Rachel clutched Anna's arm. "You didn't tell the truth about what?"

"About Eva being interested in a young man," Anna admitted softly.

"Are you saying she does have a young man?"

Anna nodded. "*Jah.* She didn't want you to know because he's not Amish. She met him in town while he was visiting." Anna paused. "He is older than she."

Shock showed on Rachel's face. She clutched her hands to her chest. "Have you met him? How long has she been seeing this man?" Noah asked.

"*Nay.* I haven't met him. And Eva didn't know him for long. A few days, perhaps."

Noah wrote down what Anna said. "Do you know his name?"

Anna shook her head. "She wouldn't tell me. She said he worried about others trying to keep them apart."

Noah's heart sank. "Did she tell you where they would meet up?"

Anna's next answer was disappointing. "She wouldn't say. I advised her not to see this man again. If he wanted her to sneak around—keep things from her family—he is not a *gut* person."

"Did she mention meeting this man last night?" Walker spoke up.

Tears glistened in Anna's eyes. "I do not know. Eva stopped telling me about meeting him when I advised her against seeing him again. Do you think this man did something to her? Should I have tried to stop her?"

"You didn't do anything wrong, Anna," Noah said. If

Eva was supposed to meet this man, why was her purse found on the side of the road? Unless Eva realized something was wrong and struggled with her kidnapper. The purse may have been left behind in the kidnapper's rush to get Eva out of sight.

Rachel's gaze clung to Noah's, desperate for assurances. He did his best not to show his fears while praying Eva's foolish mistake wouldn't end up costing the young Amish woman her life.

SEVEN

"I'll be there with you at all times," Noah assured Rachel. He reached for her hand and squeezed it. "How long have you worked at Christner's Bulk Foods Store?" He kept his attention on the road ahead.

Rachel studied his handsome profile. The tiny lines around his eyes and mouth reminded her the carefree Noah of their childhood was gone. Once again, she wondered about his life now. Had he been in love? The thought hurt, but she had no right to feel this way. She'd married Daniel during Noah's first year at university.

"Rachel?"

The tips of her ears burned with embarrassment at being caught staring. She cleared her throat. "Almost a year now. Since Daniel's death." Her world had collapsed when she'd learned her husband had not survived the accident. Then the baby died, too. Barely three months pregnant, she'd lost her last piece of Daniel and so much more.

Noah's hands tightened on the wheel. "Losing your husband must have been hard. It's difficult to lose someone you care about."

His words settled into her heart like a knife. He spoke like someone who knew firsthand the pain of such a loss.

The questions she wanted to ask would not come. She was grateful when Noah pulled up in front of the bulk foods store.

He checked his watch. "Almost eight." Time to open the store.

He studied the dark store before exiting the vehicle. Rachel did the same before handing him the key to the store. He unlocked the shop. As soon as they were inside, he relocked the door.

"What are you doing?" she asked, her heart pounding. Had he seen something?

"I'm going to check around the store first. Once things are secured, we'll unlock it."

Rachel drew in a breath and nodded, trying to keep the panic from taking life. At seventy, Esther Christner had suffered some health issues recently and had been forced to slow down. Rachel had agreed to manage the store for her a couple of days a week.

Esther and her husband did not have children of their own. Since Levi's death more than ten years earlier, Esther had been running the bulk foods store all by herself.

"The place is clear. It should be safe to open," Noah said when he came from the storeroom. "How many people do you see on an average day?"

Rachel unlocked the door. "It depends. If the weather is *gut*, perhaps there may be ten or more. Bad weather like this tends to keep customers away."

Noah nodded. "I'll try to be as inconspicuous as possible. You should go about your daily duties. We'll keep this as normal as possible."

She smiled at his consideration. "*Denki.* I will put on the *kaffe*. Esther likes to serve hot coffee to her customers."

Picking up the coffeepot, Rachel carried it to the small kitchen at the rear of the store and filled it. A battery-powered pump brought water to the store. All of the

Amish businesses around the community used diesel generators to power their lights.

With the coffee brewing, Rachel straightened the canned goods shelves. After double-checking their surroundings, Noah came to help.

"I might as well make myself useful," he said when she arched a brow.

While they worked, all the questions she wanted to ask plagued her, but did she really want to know he'd fallen in love with another?

"How are your parents and your sister, Cassie?" she asked instead.

A single muscle worked along his jaw. "They are doing okay, I guess. Mom and Dad moved to Texas a while back to be closer to Cassie."

His response produced more questions than it answered, but she sensed he didn't want to talk about his family. Noah was close to his mother and Cassie, but his relationship with his father had been strained in the past since his father openly opposed the time Noah spent with Rachel and his son resented the interference in his life.

Waneta Glick, one of the Amish ladies from the community, came in, and Rachel stepped to the counter to assist.

"*Ach*, good morning, Rachel. I am so happy to see the store open. I wasn't sure in such weather." Waneta glanced out the window as the snow continued to fall. "It is coming down in buckets out there."

Rachel smiled at the older woman. "It is. May I help you find something?"

"*Jah*, I am in need of something to treat a cold. Henry isn't feeling well this morning. I said he should rest, and I would take care of the chores, but you know how men are." Waneta chuckled. "Now he's feeling much worse."

"Oh, I'm sorry to hear that," Rachel said. She showed the woman to the shelf containing medicines. "I have used this one before, and it seems to work nicely." She pointed to one of the cold medicines.

"*Denki.* I'm sure this will be fine." Waneta paid for her purchase. She started to leave when she spotted Noah and stopped. "Is all well here?" she asked with a frown on her face.

Keeping the nightmare to herself was hard. "*Jah*, it is. The deputy is an old friend."

Waneta didn't appear convinced, but with one final glance Noah's way, she headed outside to the buggy parked next to Noah's patrol car. Rachel let go of a breath. She hated keeping the truth from the older woman.

The ringing of Noah's cell phone rattled along her frayed nerves. He glanced at the number, frowned and stepped away to take the call.

She watched him for a moment before turning away, in need of something to do to keep her mind occupied.

There were boxes in the storeroom that needed to be placed on the shelves. Rachel unpacked several and stacked the canned goods on a cart.

As she worked, she broke down the boxes, then carried them outside to the trash bin behind the store.

She'd barely cleared the door when someone seized her from behind. A large hand covered her mouth. She fought and kicked with all her strength, unable to call out for help.

"I have you now. This time, you're not getting away. He's waiting for you." She recognized his voice. It was the same man who broke into her home. He dragged her toward a car parked behind the store. As hard as she struggled, it was useless. He was too strong. Her kidnapper had found her, and she had no way to let Noah know what was happening.

The call could not have been more discouraging. Walker had spoken to the Stoltzfuses. They didn't recall Eva coming into the bakery with anyone. Another dead end along with the results from the search of the barn, where the crime scene unit hadn't been able to obtain any viable prints.

Noah returned the phone to his pocket and tried to keep his frustration from showing. He had to stay positive for Rachel.

He glanced around. Rachel was nowhere in sight. The rear door stood open. Dread slipped down his spine. Drawing his weapon, he ran toward the open door.

As soon as he stepped across the threshold, he spotted Rachel struggling with a man who was trying to force her toward a waiting car.

"Sheriff's department. Let her go and get your hands in the air! Now," Noah called out.

The man jerked toward Noah, his face covered in a mask like the other assailants.

"Get your hands in the air!" Noah repeated while quickly advancing on them.

Rachel's panicked gaze fastened onto him.

"That's far enough," the man yelled and pulled a gun from his pocket. "I need her. You, not at all."

Noah stopped, but kept the gun trained on the man.

"Let her go and put your weapon down."

The man pushed Rachel hard. She stumbled forward, and Noah caught her before she hit the ground. The man jumped into the car and slammed it in gear, tires squealing down the alley.

Rachel trembled as he held her close. He pulled out his

phone and immediately let Walker know about the attack. "I'm with Rachel behind the Christner Bulk Foods Store. Someone tried to kidnap her." Noah gave a description of the man and the four-door black sedan. "I have a plate number, as well." He gave it to Walker.

"Ryan's close. I'll have him intercept the man."

Ending the call, Noah held Rachel a little away. "Did he hurt you?" he asked, searching her face. He'd been so terrified when he saw the man trying to force Rachel into the car. What if he hadn't been able to stop it from happening?

"*Nay*, I am *oke*." She pulled away and straightened her prayer *kapp* and apron. "I recognized his voice. He's the one who broke into my house. He grabbed me the second I stepped outside."

Noah glanced around the alley, blaming himself for what happened. He should never have let her out of his sight. "Let's get you inside." With his hand resting against her back, he hurried her inside and quickly relocked the door.

"I don't think it's wise to stay here any longer. We need to close the store, Rachel." Before he got the words out, she rejected the idea.

"I cannot leave now. Mrs. Christner is counting on me to be here." She lifted her chin. He'd seen that same look many times in the past whenever Rachel made up her mind about something. It was pointless to argue.

While he admired her loyalty, the men targeting her knew where Rachel lived and worked, and they'd proved themselves more than capable of getting to her.

"All right, but I'm calling for backup to help watch the place. And if the weather doesn't clear soon, we're leaving before we get stuck here."

She smiled and reached for his hand. "*Denki*," she

said. The touch of her skin against his sent him to places best left alone. The first time he'd worked up the nerve to hold her hand. Their first kiss.

He linked their fingers. "I'm sorry this is happening to you."

Her emerald eyes held on to his, reclaiming the piece of his heart she would always own. As much as he wished he could rewrite history, it was impossible. He'd made so many mistakes in life. Believing his father instead of his heart. Olivia's death.

The argument he'd started that ultimately caused her to storm out of the house. He couldn't even remember what it had been about anymore. Only its consequences. Olivia had told him she was finished with him. At the time, he hadn't cared. With an unexpected storm dumping snow on the remote mountain area, Noah should have stopped her, or at least gone after her. Anger and pride had kept him home, and Olivia had driven off the side of the mountain to her death.

He carried the guilt of her death with him each day. He'd hit rock bottom. When Walker invited him to church, Noah had agreed to go. God met him at that tiny church and changed his life. Yet he hadn't been able to forgive himself for his part in Olivia's death.

Swallowing deep, he let Rachel go and stepped back. The mistakes he'd made were there to remind him he'd messed so many things up. Hurt people, including Rachel. He couldn't do that to her again. Rachel deserved so much more than the damaged man standing before her now.

EIGHT

She turned away, Noah's rejection just as stinging as it had been seven years earlier. An awkward silence she could not associate with them stood between them. Rachel struggled to think of something to say and was grateful it proved unnecessary with the arrival of deputies Ryan and Cole.

"Any news on the car?" Noah asked once they closed the door.

Ryan shook his head. "I'm guessing he's familiar with the back roads. Which seems to indicate he either lives here now or has in the past."

The news couldn't have been more discouraging.

"I doubt that he will try anything more here after what happened, but I'd feel better having you two close," Noah told them.

"No problem," Cole said. "We'll pull around behind the store and out of sight."

When it was the two of them again, Noah came over to her, the intensity in his eyes leaving her breathless. "You can't give up. Eva needs you to stay strong."

Tears were close, and she couldn't stop them. She'd grown up believing in peace and harmony. She didn't understand violence. He brushed the tears away with his thumb. "We'll figure it out," he said gently. "We'll get her back." She needed to believe him.

"I spoke to Walker earlier. He talked to the Stoltzfuses.

They haven't seen Eva in a while, certainly not with anyone. In other words, we don't know who she was meeting with or even if it happened."

"Do you think this man she met is A. Miller?" Rachel couldn't believe Eva had kept something this big secret from her.

"It's possible. Walker is running the name through our system to see if anything comes up."

"What do you think happened to her?" she forced herself to ask because she had to know. Though six years separated them, she and Eva had always been close. She felt Eva in her heart whenever they were apart. Since her sister's disappearance, that connection was no longer as strong.

"I wish I could give you the answers you need. Eva is a strong girl. She won't give up. I need you not to either."

She would never give up on her sister.

Outside, the snow continued to pile up on the road. Clouds completely obscured the mountains in the distance. Rachel shivered as a chill that had nothing to do with the cold bored down deep.

With several hours left before the store closed, Rachel rolled out the cart she'd loaded with canned goods and took them to the shelves.

She and Noah worked to put away the food, yet all Rachel could think about was her sister. She'd been so busy dealing with her own pain that she hadn't realized Eva was changing. Growing up. Though her sister seemed content with her life, Rachel wondered if that was an act. Had discontent made Eva reach out to an *Englisch* man?

Hours passed without a single customer and the weather continued to deteriorate. Rachel agreed it was time to close up the store.

Noah let the deputies know they were leaving while Rachel shut off the coffee and lights and locked up the store.

"The snow's not letting up any," Noah said as they stepped out into the blizzard. Darkness came early at this time of the year in the shadows of the mountains. Twilight settled around them.

They headed out of the town while Noah kept his speed low on the precarious road. Rachel noticed headlights behind them, and whipped around in her seat.

Noah covered her hand. "That's Ryan and Cole. They'll be watching the house along with me."

She swallowed and faced the front. There would be police officers close by throughout the night. She was safe.

Reaching her turnoff, Noah eased the car down the drive. The dark house appeared in the headlights' beam. Her home. Would she ever feel safe here again?

"Lock up behind me. I'll take a walk through the house before you go inside."

He exited and she locked the doors. Noah clicked on his flashlight. Headlights reflected in the side mirror. The second patrol car pulled up next to her. Both deputies got out. Cole headed around the side of the house while Ryan started for the barn.

Through the curtained windows, Noah's flashlight skipped around each of the rooms. After what felt like ages, he came outside to get her.

"There's no sign of anyone being here. Let's get you inside and out of the cold."

She stepped across the threshold to the warmth of the living room. Noah had made a fire.

Removing her cloak and traveling bonnet, Rachel wasn't sure what to do with herself. Usually, she and Eva would prepare the evening meal together.

She headed into the kitchen and lit the lantern on the

table. Standing in the middle of the room, Rachel rubbed her hands over her arms. The cold pierced down to her very heart.

Noah warmed his hands by the woodstove. The lanky young boy she'd known before was all grown up.

He looked up and caught her watching. Rachel's chest tightened painfully and she turned away. Having him here in her home reminded her of all her foolish dreams. The ones that would never be possible for them.

"All's clear," Cole told him. "To be safe, Ryan and I will set up closer to the house. We can tuck the patrol car in there—" he pointed to the woods out front "—and still have a good view of the house and yard."

"That should work," Noah said. "If anything jumps off, call my cell phone. The radio isn't secure. He could be monitoring our transmissions."

"Will do." Cole and Ryan headed out to their patrol vehicle.

Rachel stood close to the fire, watching him.

"There's been no sign of the men," Noah assured her.

She sighed. "So what will happen now?"

"We wait. If he tries something, we're ready for him." The panic on her face told him she wouldn't sleep well. "Relax, Rachel. You have some of the best law enforcement officers around protecting you."

She ducked her head. "I know, but it's hard. All I can think about is Eva."

Though Noah was close to his sister, Cassie, since she'd moved to Texas they didn't see each other all that much. Mostly because his dad was there. "I know it's hard. I remember how close you two were," he said quietly.

"Do you think she's still alive?" She held his gaze while he struggled to keep his doubts to himself.

"I do. The way these men keep coming after you, they need both you and Eva for a reason. They'll keep her alive until they can get you, and that's not going to happen."

Hope dawned on her pretty face, and he prayed he hadn't just lied to her. There was no proof except a gut feeling that told him both sisters were essential to whatever diabolical plan these men had.

"Are you hungry?" she asked. "It has been hours since we ate, and I have some ham-and-noodle casserole leftover."

He recalled how Beth used to make the casserole for him because she knew how much he loved it. "I haven't had ham-and-noodle casserole since your mom's."

Rachel smiled at the memory. "She loved making it for you, for sure. *Mamm* was always crazy about you."

He'd spent many an hour with Beth and Ezra. Loved how they included him as if he were part of the family.

"She's a special lady," he said.

Rachel took the casserole out and placed it in the oven to warm. Soon, the aroma of ham and cheese took him to happier times.

Over the years, he'd thought about dropping by to visit Rachel's family, but the way things ended between him and Rachel made it awkward, especially after she married.

"What about Cole and Ryan? Should we call them in?" Rachel asked, and Noah shook his head.

"I'll take them each a plate."

When the food was hot, Rachel dished helpings onto plates and Noah carried them to the table. Once they were both seated, he bowed his head and poured his heart out to God. Being amongst Amish people, seeing Rachel again, brought up all the old longings of his heart. He'd loved this way of life once. Thought about embracing their faith. He'd given up on that dream when his father moved the family away.

Lord, I need Your help. Direct my life. Help me to make wise decisions. As much as I want to let the anger I have toward my father go, it's hard. I need You.

When his prayer ended, he glanced up and found Rachel watching him. Had she seen the longings that inundated his heart?

He dug into the casserole, unable to acknowledge the questions he saw in her eyes.

Noah ate in silence while Rachel barely touched her food.

"Why don't you try and get some rest?" he suggested. "You look ready to drop."

"I managed to sleep last night." He had a feeling it was about as much as he'd gotten. A couple of hours at best.

"Still, you should try. I'll clean up and take some food to Cole and Ryan."

Her grateful smiled warmed his heart. That she didn't protest proved he'd been right.

With the dishes washed, he took two covered plates out to his friends.

As he stepped off the porch, something caught his attention and Noah stopped midstride. Was that a light in the woods to the side of house?

Sitting the plates on the porch, Noah called Cole immediately. "There's someone in the woods."

A second passed before Cole said, "I see it. Looks like they're heading behind the house. We're on it."

"I'll wait with Rachel."

"Roger that," Cole said and ended the call.

Noah went back inside and locked the door. As much as he wanted to be part of the search, he didn't dare leave Rachel alone.

The hair on Noah's arms stood at attention. He crept to the front window and caught sight of something. Before he had time to process what was happening, the door crashed open. A man dressed entirely in black, his face covered with a mask, charged Noah, swinging what appeared to be a board. Before Noah could dodge, the man slammed it against his temple. Pain exploded from the contact point. Noah fell to his knees. His vision distorted.

Rachel!

The man dropped the board and headed toward the back of the house. Noah stumbled to his feet and went after the man on unsteady legs. Before the man could open Rachel's bedroom door, Noah slammed into him. He staggered into the door and slid across the wall.

With his vision still blurry, Noah reached for the man and hauled him up to his feet. He slugged him hard. The man's head flew sideways. Before Noah could get in another punch, the man smashed his fist against Noah's jaw, knocking him backward.

At a disadvantage, the man punched Noah in the midsection. The breath whooshed from his body. Noah doubled over. From somewhere outside, voices carried into the house. Cole and Ryan were close.

With one final look at Noah, his attacker bounded for the open door.

His breathing labored, Noah grabbed his cell phone. "He was just in here. He's getting away," Noah said when Cole picked up.

"We're almost to the house."

Noah shoved the phone into his pocket and tried to clear away the cobwebs.

These men were just going to keep coming until they had Rachel. Something was important enough for them to risk jail if not death to get to her. Noah had to figure it out soon. Because the next time, they might succeed.

NINE

The noise of a scuffle outside her door shot her out of bed. What was happening?

Crossing the room, she listened. Silence. Rachel opened the door. A shadowy figure came toward her. She screamed. Someone clutched her arms.

"It's okay, Rachel. It's me." Relief made her knees weak.

"What happened? I heard a noise."

"Someone broke in." She noticed blood trickling from a plum-size knot forming on the side of his head.

"You're hurt," she exclaimed.

"I'm okay." But he didn't appear so. Noah slumped down into the closest rocker.

Rachel quickly closed and locked the door.

Moving to his side, she gently examined the wound.

He winced and pulled her hand away. "I'm okay."

She sank to the empty rocker and couldn't stop trembling. Someone had been in her house again. "They are not going to stop, are they?"

Noah opened his eyes and looked at her. "There's no way I'm going to let them hurt you again."

As she peered deep into his eyes, she wanted to believe him, but these men had proven to be more than determined.

He touched her cheek. "I know this feels like an impossible situation, but we will find out what's truly going on. I just need you to trust me."

The sincerity on his face made her believe he would move mountains to protect her and bring Eva home. But would it be enough?

Something shifted in his eyes. He appeared so serious. Her breath lodged in her throat. Feelings she thought were just part of a childhood fantasy resurfaced.

Having him close made the past and what might have been impossible to face. If Noah hadn't left her, would they have married? Had children of their own? It was too painful to consider. She would probably never know what it felt like to be called *Mamm* by a *kinna*.

A knock sounded at the front door, and Noah's hand fell away. When he went to answer it, she could breathe again. The past had no place between them anymore, but part of her didn't want to let it go.

Cole and Ryan stood in the entrance. With a glance back at her, Noah stepped out onto the porch.

Touching her hands to her heated cheeks, Rachel stirred the fire and added a couple of logs for warmth. She had to find a way to deal with her feelings for Noah. There could be no future for them. He was not Amish… and she was damaged goods. Noah deserved a wife that could bear him children. Not someone like her.

She'd loved Daniel, but in a different way. They'd shared so many beautiful years together, yet through all the happy memories, the accident stood out in her mind. She'd never forget that dreadful day.

Tears were close. They always were whenever she thought about Daniel and the baby.

"Are you okay?" Noah asked from the doorway. She hadn't realized he'd returned. Rachel scrubbed the back of her hand over her eyes before facing him. He came in and closed the door.

"*Jah*, I am fine." But nothing could be further from the truth, and she was grateful Noah accepted her answer without prying.

"There was no sign of him."

Despair rose inside of her, and she fought to keep it down. "What do we do now?"

"It's not safe to stay here any longer."

Her heart sank. She would be forced to leave her home. For how long?

"I know it's not ideal, but you will be safer. I spoke to Walker, and he suggested you stay with him and his wife. They have a spread a little ways from here. It's beautiful there and secluded. I will be there the entire time."

Pulling in a breath, she asked, "When do we need to leave?"

"As soon as you can be ready." He held her gaze. "We'll make sure no one follows us, and you'll love Theresa. She's like a mother to all of us deputies."

She forced a smile. Noah was trying to make the best of things, and she should try, as well. "She sounds nice."

He held her gaze. So many questions needed answering in her heart. She'd give anything to know why he'd left her when she was younger without so much as a word. But now was not the time.

Rachel cleared her throat. "I'll go pack." Without waiting for an answer, she hurried to her room. Closing the door softly, she wondered if there would ever be a time when she and Noah could move beyond what happened in their past and be friends.

Noah kept his attention on the road ahead while periodically checking the rearview mirror. So far, no one had followed them. He prayed that wouldn't change. Cole and Ryan would make sure they weren't tailed. Megan and Aden would take over their watch and return to Rachel's house. The fewer deputies around Walker's place to draw attention to it the better. If the men chasing them proved true to form, they'd return to Rachel's house looking for her.

He could feel Rachel watching him. He knew he'd been quiet, but his soul was troubled.

"When did Cassie get married and move to Texas?" she asked when he couldn't think of anything to say.

"About three years ago. She and her husband live near Austin now. My parents moved there when Cassie's little girl was born."

"Your parents must be pleased to have a granddaughter to dote on," she prompted when he fell silent.

Keeping his voice from reflecting his emotions was hard. Every time he spoke about his father, the anger was still there. "I guess so."

He snuck a quick look her way. That frown line had appeared again between her eyes. "Do you keep in touch with them?" She kept her attention on his face.

A breath escaped before he answered. "I call them a couple times a month. Mom mostly answers. My dad and I don't see eye to eye on a lot of things, including what he thinks is best for my life." The bitterness in his tone was evident and he hated it.

The argument they'd had when his father informed him the family was moving to Eagle's Nest was always close at mind. He'd felt as if his world ended. He loved Rachel, and he'd tried to make his dad see the truth, but his father insisted Noah would end up hurting Rachel in the long run if he stayed with her. He'd grow tired of the Amish way of life in time. Where would that leave Rachel? Noah had allowed his father to get into his head. Convince him leaving her was the right decision. For a while, he'd believed his father.

After he'd been away at the university for about a year, Isaac told him Rachel had married. That's when Noah's rebellion had reached another level. Rarely coming home, his grades suffered. Then he'd met Olivia. Noah knew he didn't love her. He was trying to get back at his father for interfering in his life. After Olivia's death, the chasm between him and his father widened.

When his parents moved to Texas it made things easier. No more awkward holiday meals. Noah used the excuse of work to keep from visiting whenever possible.

Yet since he'd started attending church, God was convicting him of his bad behavior toward his dad. Noah knew he needed to set things right between them. He just wasn't sure how.

Beside him, Rachel appeared restless. "You okay?" he asked, rousing himself from his troubled thoughts.

She shook her head. "Not really. I'm trying to make sense of what's happening. Why do you think they want us so badly?"

To that, he had no answer. "Nothing about it makes sense. You and your family live a simple life. As far as you know, there's no one holding a grudge?"

Surprised flickered in her eyes. "Why would someone have a grudge? We are rarely in the *Englisch* world." She lifted her palms. "I can't understand any of this."

Neither could he. "If they were after money, I think we would have received a ransom request by now. It's safe to say, this isn't about extorting money from your family." Frowning, he focused on the road again. "So far, we've run into nothing but dead ends in our search to identify A. Miller."

A sigh escaped her lips. "I know everyone in our community, Noah. He is not from here." Rachel had lived her entire life in the West Kootenai community, and it was a small one, with a single church district.

"We've expanded our search for Miller to outside the community. He could be an *Englischer* who lives in the county. Hopefully, something will turn up soon from the expanded search."

She brushed a hand across her cheek. Her tears melted his heart.

Noah took her hand and held it as a sob escaped. He'd give anything to have some news of comfort.

He spotted the turnoff to Walker's ranch and pulled in. The gate had a keypad lock. Noah rolled the window down and punched in the correct code.

When the gate opened, he drove through. The house sat some distance from the road, secured from sight by a thickly wooded area filled with spruce and ponderosa pines.

The woods cleared and the log home came into view. He'd spent many recent holidays here with Walker and Theresa, pouring his heart out to Theresa. She knew all about the way he'd once cared for Rachel. She had been the one to urge him to reach out to Rachel after Daniel passed away, believing if Noah ever stood a chance at having a future with someone, he'd need to settle his past. Yet his demons wouldn't let him. He'd hurt Rachel by leaving the way he had. She wouldn't want to hear from him.

He stopped the car out front and shifted toward Rachel, seeing the anxiousness on her face. "Relax. Theresa will be mothering you in no time."

When she didn't answer, he opened the door and came around to her side. Rachel climbed out next to him. Noah took the bag she held.

The front door opened and both Theresa and Walker came out.

Noah stepped up onto the porch with Rachel.

"Theresa, this is Rachel Albrecht." He introduced her to the older woman.

Rachel extended her hand, but Theresa ignored it and enveloped Rachel in a hug. Theresa was a hugger who never met a stranger.

"Come inside and warm up."

Theresa took the bag from Noah, and she and Rachel went in, leaving Noah and Walker alone on the porch.

"This is hitting a little too close for comfort," Walker said when it was just the two of them. "So far, we have nothing to go on to locate the girl, and we have no idea what these men have planned for her or Rachel. We need to find Eva and fast because I'm afraid her time is running out."

Noah couldn't let that happen. Eva had her whole life ahead of her. And Rachel had lost so much already. He wouldn't let her lose her sister, as well. No matter what, he'd do everything in his power to bring Eva home safely. Even if he had to give his life for hers.

TEN

"I've made up a room for you next to ours," Theresa told her. "Let's sit for a bit."

Rachel followed her to the sofa placed near an enormous rock fireplace.

"Are you hungry, hon?" the woman asked.

Food was the last thing on Rachel's mind. "No, thank you," she said and glanced toward the door, feeling Noah's absence deeply. With him, she felt safe.

Theresa smiled kindly. "They'll be a few minutes. No doubt they're discussing what happened at your house tonight."

Rachel met the woman's gaze. "I'm sorry to intrude on your life like this. I hope it's not too much of an inconvenience."

Theresa patted her arm. "Not at all. We're happy to have you here." Theresa hesitated. "I know you're worried about your sister, about your own life, but you have some of the best people working round the clock to solve this case. If I were in trouble, I can't think of anyone I'd rather have on my side than Walker and his team."

The honesty on the older woman's face helped her to relax. "I know they are doing everything they can to find Eva."

Theresa held her gaze. "I understand you and Noah knew each other when you were younger."

Rachel's eyes widened. She had no idea Noah had spoken about her.

She lowered her head. "We were neighbors…and good friends. Noah always looked out for me growing up."

"He's like that, helping out those in need. I think what happened with Olivia has left its mark on him. Makes him want to try his best to save people."

Color drained from Rachel's face. "Olivia?"

"Noah's wife," Theresa said without looking away. Rachel couldn't hide her surprise. She'd been right. Noah had loved someone else.

"Her dying hurt him badly. But that was a long time ago," Theresa said with a sigh. "And he's grown up so much. It's time he remarried. Noah deserves to be happy again. Have a family of his own."

Each word struck like a blow. A family. Something she could never give him.

"Oh, it's after midnight. You must be exhausted. Why don't I show you to your room?" Theresa rose and Rachel did the same.

Grabbing her bag, Theresa headed down the hallway and stopped next to one of the doors. Opening it, she went inside. "This was our oldest daughter's room. Candace lives in Billings with her husband and two daughters now. I think you should be comfortable enough here." She placed the bag on the bed. "There's a bathroom next door with towels. If you need anything at all, you let me know."

Rachel nodded. "*Denki*, Theresa, you are very kind."

Theresa stopped beside her. "I can see you're important to Noah, and he's like a son to Walker and me." She touched Rachel's hand. "Get some sleep and try not to worry too much. They'll figure this out." Stepping out of the room, Theresa shut the door quietly.

With a tiny sigh, Rachel sank to the bed's softness. She still couldn't believe Noah had been married. In her mind, she tried to envision the type of woman he would love. No doubt, she would be beautiful and *Englisch*. Olivia, a pretty name. It hurt so much to think of him with someone else even though she had no right to these feelings.

Grabbing her nightgown and brush, Rachel headed to the bathroom to change. As she glanced in the mirror, the woman staring back at her was almost unrecognizable. Dark smudges beneath each eye spoke of lack of sleep. Her cheeks were sunken. Fear was branded on her face.

Turning away, she went back to the bedroom and removed her prayer *kapp*, unpinning her hair to brush out the tangles.

The curtains above the window were open. A shiver sped down Rachel's spine as a sense of being watched made her click off the light. She set down the brush and peered out into the night, her imagination taking her to terrifying places. The feeling of being watched wouldn't go away.

Yanking the curtains closed, she flipped on the light and the darkness fled.

Her hands unsteady, Rachel brought out her Bible and read a favorite verse.

And the peace of God, which passeth all understanding, shall keep your hearts and minds through Christ Jesus.

If ever she needed *Gott*'s peace it was now. She bowed her head. "Holy Father, keep Eva safe. Please help Noah find the people responsible for taking her and bring my sister back home to her family."

A breath slipped from her lips and peace that only came from *Gott* enveloped her like a warm winter's cloak.

Outside the room, she heard voices quietly talking. Noah and Walker. Rachel pulled the covers back and slipped into the bed, the soft sheets welcoming. As she closed her eyes troubled thoughts plagued her mind. Foremost was Noah. At one time she thought she knew him better than anyone. She'd been wrong. The grown-up Noah held many secrets.

Noah's eyes flew open, and he sat up in bed and listened. Nothing but quiet. Yet something had jarred him out of light sleep.

Seconds ticked by before he realized it wasn't a sound that had woken him but a scent. Smoke filled the room. The house was on fire.

Lunging from the bed, he cracked the door open. A wall of smoke billowed inside. Covering his mouth with his hand, Noah crouched low to the ground and eased from the room. Rachel was in the room next to his. He went inside and hurried to the bed.

She sat up. "What's happening?" she asked in a breathless tone.

"The house is on fire. We have to wake the others and get out." She threw the covers off and followed him to the door.

"Cover your mouth and nose and stay low," he said. Rachel reached for her prayer *kapp* and held it against her nose. "Grab on to me and stay close. It's hard to see through the smoke."

She clutched his shirt. They'd taken but a few steps when Noah spotted Walker and Theresa emerging from their room.

"Where's the fire's origin?" Walker got out through a fit of coughing. He held his wife close. Theresa pressed her face against her husband's shoulder.

The smoke sent tears streaming from Noah's eyes. He pointed to the curtains billowing in the living room. "I'm guessing they threw a Molotov cocktail through the window. They're trying to force us outside. They're planning an attack." Flames licked up the living room walls.

A noise at the back door drew Noah's attention. The men were trying to break through.

Rachel clutched his hand.

"The window in our room. It's the only way. We can climb out and drop down behind the house," Walker told them.

"There's not much time," Noah said as the fire continued to spread.

Walker and Theresa hurried back inside their room while Noah and Rachel followed.

Noah clicked the lock on the door and shoved a chair against the knob. "That should buy us a little time."

The back door gave way. The men breached the house. Time was critical.

Shoving his gun in the waist of his pants, Walker opened the window.

Noah had no doubt the fire had been set deliberately. The men were desperate to get to Rachel. "My guess is they have more men outside waiting for us. Let me go first," he said and swung his legs out the window. The house sat on a knoll with a sloping backyard, which meant the drop would be steep. One false move could end in a twisted ankle.

Using his arms, he shifted so that his body hung over the side. Noah dangled for a moment before dropping to the ground. Hitting hard, his legs almost buckled beneath him.

The wind howled around the edge of the house, carrying with it a wealth of snow flurries. A winter storm was hitting the mountains. The wind had the potential to spread the fire. They needed help now.

With a quick look around, Noah motioned to Walker, who helped Rachel out the window.

The terror on her face ripped at his heart. "Don't look at the ground, stay focused on me. I have you."

After slipping down the side of the house as far as possible, Rachel let go and Noah caught her in his arms.

"You're okay," he said and sat her on her feet, then focused on the burning house. Where were the men?

Walker glanced behind him. "Smoke's filling the room pretty fast. We don't have much time. Hurry, Theresa." Walker helped his wife onto the ledge.

Theresa jumped, barely giving Noah enough time to catch her.

Once she was safe beside Rachel, Walker hit the ground. Losing his footing, he stumbled and fell.

Theresa rushed to her husband's side. "Are you okay?"

Noah could see, right away, Walker had reinjured an old knee wound. "I'm calling for backup and I'll get the fire department dispatched right away." Grabbing his phone, Noah made the call. He explained to Janine what had happened.

"Aden and Megan are still at Rachel's house. I'll send them over. I'm calling the fire department now. Are you all safe?"

Noah glanced at the raging fire. He had no idea, but he had a bad feeling. "For now," he told her.

"Be careful, Noah. These are some bad guys. I'm praying for you all."

Ending the call, Noah pocketed the phone. Cold settled in deep. "We need to find someplace safe to get out of this storm and out of sight. I don't like being in the open like this. We'll be easy targets out here."

Walker pointed to the barn a little ways behind the house. "We should be safe enough in there until our backup arrives."

"Hurry," Noah urged, his gut telling him whoever set the fire was close and ready to make their next move.

They eased away from the heat. To the left, Walker had cleared the land for pasture. Trees flanked the right side. Noah kept his body between Rachel and the woods.

"You and Theresa head for the barn," Noah yelled over the noise of the storm and fire. "Walker and I will hold off the men inside."

Rachel hesitated. She didn't want to leave him.

"Go, we'll be okay," he assured her.

Theresa reached for Rachel's arm and together they raced to the building.

The women reached the barn when gunfire exploded nearby. The men had left the house and were coming after them. Noah returned fire, forcing the shooters to take cover in the woods nearby.

A lull in the firefight gave Noah time to shove his backup mag into the Glock 9mm. The magazine held seventeen rounds, but it was his last one. "Let's get out of here before they start shooting again." The words had barely cleared his lips when another round lit up the woods.

He and Walker hit the ground together. This time bullets flew past them close enough for Noah to hear the noise they made. Their attackers were trying to kill them.

"We have to get out of the open. They're not playing around anymore," Walker yelled.

Noah rolled onto his side and fired, forcing the men to take cover.

He leaped to his feet, while Walker rose slower, favoring his injured leg. Running through blinding snow toward the open barn door, Walker's limp slowed him down considerably. Noah would not leave his commander behind. He wrapped his arm around Walker's waist and kept running. When they were less than ten feet from the barn, the men opened up again. He and Walker hit the snow-covered ground. Every moment they were out in the open like this brought them one step closer to taking a bullet.

Aiming in the direction the shots were coming from, Noah fired off more rounds, helped Walker to his feet and all but carried him to the barn. He slammed the door closed behind him.

"They'll keep coming," Walker said between labored breaths. "Let's hope Aden and Megan get here before those men charge the barn."

Glancing around, Noah tried to pull his thoughts together. Walker's enclosed tractor sat off to one side.

"Does it run?" he asked, pointing to the machine.

Walker nodded.

Hurrying to the tractor, Noah fired it up and slowly eased the machine in front of the door. It would give them a measure of protection and hopefully prevent the men from storming the barn.

Noah checked his ammo. Almost empty. They had Walker's weapon, but it wouldn't last long against the arsenal these men possessed. He hoped they could hold out long enough for his team to arrive. Aden and Megan were a good twenty minutes out under the best of conditions.

He pulled in a breath and listened beyond the raging storm. Silence.

"What are they waiting for?" Walker said. "They have us on our heels." Noah had never seen his mentor appear so worried before.

"I counted at least four shooters. They have us outmanned, but the one thing we have going for us is that they need Rachel alive. They won't shoot blind and risk killing her."

Acrid smoke began wafting under the barn door. The men were trying to smoke them out.

ELEVEN

Rachel stared in horror at the puffs of gray smoke billowing under the door. The men must have started a fire right in front of the door. It wouldn't be long before it caught. With all the hay inside, the barn would go up like a tinderbox.

"What can we do? We will die if we stay here." She searched Noah's face, seeing the worry he could not hide.

"We're going to get out of here." Noah pointed to the tractor. "And that's how we're going to do it."

He fired the machine up. "It'll be a tight squeeze with all of us, but it's our only chance."

"What's your plan?" Walker asked as he watched the door go up in a blaze. "We can't go out the door. We'll be heading straight into the fire they set. It's too risky."

"Does this thing have enough horsepower to break down a wall?" Noah asked.

Walker's expression was not reassuring. "We're about to find out."

Noah helped Rachel inside, followed by Theresa. He climbed into the driver's seat. When Walker ambled up the steps and closed the door, there was barely room to breathe much less move.

The fire quickly engulfed the front of the building. Walker pointed behind them. "Try for the rear wall.

There's some damage to the building there from last winter's storm. It'll be your best shot."

Putting the tractor in gear, Noah started down the narrow path between bales of hay. As he neared the wall, he raised the front loader bucket into the air.

"Hang on," Noah warned as they hit the wall hard.

The force threw Rachel forward. She caught herself before hitting the windshield. When the shuddering impact stopped, the wall remained intact.

"Try it again," Walker said, glancing behind them. Their window of escape was quickly slipping away.

Noah backed up a bit, then drove forward as fast as the tractor would allow. It smashed against the wall hard, but the structure didn't budge.

"It's useless. There's only one way out of here. We have to brave the fire." Noah clasped Rachel's hand. She slowly nodded.

"They'll be waiting for us," Walker said. "Expect a firefight, and this thing isn't bulletproof."

Turning the tractor around in the tight space proved challenging, but once he managed it, Noah drove toward the raging fire while Rachel squeezed her eyes shut. She couldn't watch.

"Hang on. I'm going to try to get through it as fast as I can." Noah floored the accelerator.

She felt the heat from the fire as they entered the inferno. The tractor plowed through the compromised entrance while pieces of debris rained down on it. Would the fuel tank ignite?

Holy Father, please protect us. The simple prayer slipped through her mind. Noah didn't stop.

"We're out," he exclaimed when they'd left the blazing barn behind.

She opened her eyes. In front of them, the house was

engulfed. Behind them, the barn crumbled in flames. Bile rose in her throat. Because of her, Walker and Theresa had lost so much.

Four men stepped out in front of them, weapons aimed. Noah jerked the tractor right and kept going.

"It's a risk, but I believe they can't afford to shoot at us now and chance hitting you," Noah said to Rachel.

She looked behind them. "They're running after us."

Passing the house, Noah headed out into a cleared field. "Where does this lead?" he asked Walker.

"Eventually back to the main highway, but there's a lot of rough terrain in between."

"We have to keep going. I'm almost out of rounds, and you're in no condition for a battle."

Walker held his wife close. Theresa was a real mountain woman. Walker had mentioned many times that she was a better shot than him. The fear Noah saw in her now drove home how dangerous their situation was.

Rachel clutched his arm as the tractor bounced across uneven ground. Thick snow continued to fall, making it impossible to see much in front of them despite the headlights.

"Look." Rachel tapped his shoulder, and he followed her gaze behind them. Red-and-blue lights flashed across the night sky. Help had arrived.

Walker twisted so he could see. "I don't see the men who attacked us. I'm guessing they fled the minute they spotted the police vehicles approaching. Let's turn this thing around."

Noah was happy to oblige. As they drew near the house once more, the Eagle's Nest Fire Department rolled onto the scene. As much as Noah hated to admit it, there was little left to save.

He stopped the tractor, and Walker slowly lumbered down. The awkward position he'd been in hadn't helped the leg's swelling any.

Theresa reached her husband's side and put her arm around his waist to help him along.

Climbing down, Noah held his hand out to Rachel. Her green eyes appeared huge against her pale skin as she stared up at the house.

He read all her thoughts and tugged her close. "This isn't your fault. You didn't ask for any of this. Don't take on that blame."

Her gaze shifted to him, shock likely preventing what he said from sinking in.

He and Rachel went over to where Walker spoke with Megan.

"Did you see them?" Noah asked. The grim expression on Megan's face was answer enough.

Megan shook her head. "No, I'm sorry. I'm guessing they had a vehicle stashed somewhere and took off." She crooked her thumb behind them. "Aden is checking the woods now."

If this followed the same pattern, Noah doubted he'd find anything useful.

While Walker ran through the events of the evening, Noah kept a careful eye on Rachel. She silently watched the firemen try to put out the fire. He was worried about her.

Theresa went over and wrapped her arms around Rachel's shoulders. "Don't you even think about blaming yourself. Those men are the ones who did this, not you, and I won't hear of it any other way."

Rachel bottom lip quivered. "But your home…it's destroyed. I am so sorry."

"It's a place to lay our heads, nothing more. We'll rebuild. The memories are in here." Theresa pointed to her heart. "We're all safe. That's what matters."

Noah knew that no matter what Theresa said, Rachel was the type of woman who would carry the guilt with her for a long time.

"You should get Rachel out of here and someplace safe," Walker said.

There was only one place Noah could think of now. The sheriff's station in Eagle's Nest. He told Walker.

"That works. Take Megan with you in case you run into trouble. As soon as this is under control, I'll call in Ryan and Cole and we'll run through the details we know so far. The attacks are escalating. I have a feeling none of us are going to be getting much sleep for a while."

On the way to the car, Noah filled Megan in.

Megan got in the back seat, while Noah held the door open for Rachel. She slipped past him without a word. He wasn't sure how much more she could take.

As he got in beside her, Rachel leaned against the headrest, eyes closed, fingers kneading the area around her temples. More than anything, he wished he could ease her worries, but after what happened here tonight, he feared the nightmare was just beginning.

Putting the car in gear, Noah slowly eased down the drive, his thoughts swirling around what happened.

The rearview mirror reflected nothing but blackness. In front, the storm raged with renewed force, plastering more snow than the wipers could handle.

Why were the kidnappers so determined? The two men had indicated they were coming after Rachel for money, yet it was established Rachel's family had nothing of value besides the land the family owned. He thought about Beth. Last he checked, there had been no suspicious activity where she was staying.

He cast a quick look Megan's way. "Any word from the sheriff in Alamosa?"

Rachel's eyes flew open and she turned toward him. "Do you think they will come after *Mamm*?"

Noah squeezed her arm. "No, probably not. I'm simply covering all bases."

"There have been no incidents reported, and the sheriff has two deputies sitting on the house," Megan said.

Noah returned to his thoughts. If the men weren't coming after Beth, then whatever this was about centered solely on Eva and Rachel…which sent them back to square one. He expelled a breath. These men wanted something bad enough to risk imprisonment to gain it. And if they didn't figure out what that was soon, he worried that the Lincoln County Sheriff's Department might not have enough manpower to stand against what was coming next.

TWELVE

Rachel stared up at the building. In the past, on the rare occasions when she made the trip to Eagle's Nest, she'd driven the buggy past the sheriff's station without giving much thought to what the men and women inside did each day. Now she knew firsthand.

While Megan went inside, Noah got out and came around to Rachel's side. Opening the door, he knelt close and enveloped her hands in his. "I know this has been a rough night, but you'll be safe here and I promise we'll catch the people behind this. We'll bring Eva home. Don't give up, Rachel. I need you to trust me."

Rachel ducked her head. She wanted to, but he'd hurt her before.

"I realize I've never told you this, Rachel, but I'm sorry about what happened between us before," he whispered, and her head shot up.

Did she really want to hear his regrets? "It no longer matters," she murmured without looking at him. "That was a long time ago."

"It matters to me," he said earnestly. "I want you to know leaving was never my choice."

Her eyes widened as she looked at his solemn face. "I don't understand."

He stared up at the sky. The storm's intensity hadn't weakened. "Let's go inside. It's freezing out here."

Neither had escaped the fire with more than the clothes

on their backs. She glanced down at her nightgown and bare feet.

"Janine's on duty. I'll see if she has something you can wear for now." He rocked to his feet and held out his hand.

Hesitating, she accepted it and stepped up next to him. Noah closed the door with her hand still tucked in his. She needed his strength more than ever because she felt like she was drowning in doubts.

As soon as they entered the station, Janine bustled their way. "Are you two all right?"

Rachel could not get words to come out of her mouth.

"We're okay," Noah answered for her. "It's just been a rough night. Do you happen to have any extra clothing here at the station Rachel could borrow?"

Janine's brows shot up as she eyed Rachel. "Oh, hon, I'm sorry. I should have realized. I do have a dress I wore to church the other day. When I had to work a shift afterward, I changed here. Let me get it for you. I think I have some sneakers that might fit you, as well," she said, noticing Rachel's bare feet.

Noah smiled at the woman's kindness. "Janine, you're prepared for anything. I knew we could count on you."

When it was just the two of them again, all Rachel could think about was his apology.

"Noah," she whispered, drawing his attention to her. The look in his eyes stole her breath away.

"What is it?" he asked.

She swallowed and gathered her courage. Before she could ask what her heart needed to know, Janine returned.

"Here you go," Janine said. They jumped apart like a couple of guilty teenagers. The older woman glanced from one to the other, a glint of curiosity in her eyes, while heat crept into Rachel's cheeks.

"You are such a petite little thing, but I think if you tie

the belt real tight it will be okay." Rachel barely caught what Janine said. All she could think about was Noah.

Janine handed Rachel the simple deep green dress and sneakers. "Oh, and I brought you my sweater. It's cold in here."

"Denki," Rachel managed.

"You are welcome. The restroom is through there."

Without answering, Rachel carried the dress to the restroom and closed the door. Leaning against it, she shut her eyes. Was it possible she'd been wrong about Noah all these years?

With a sigh, she moved away from the door. None of it mattered anymore.

She stared at herself in the mirror. Several strands of her hair had come loose from the bun she'd managed with the help of a ponytail holder borrowed from Megan. The prayer *kapp* she'd hastily tied in place during the drive to the station was covered in soot, as was her flannel gown. Smudges covered one of her cheeks. The extent of what they'd all gone through shone in her eyes.

Turning away, she slipped into one of the stalls to change. She removed her gown and pulled the dress on. Looping the matching belt around her waist, she snugged it. Rachel slipped her feet into the sneakers and laced them up. The room was cold, so she put on the sweater and left the stall.

The green color made her skin appear pale, her eyes huge pools against it. She washed her face and then untied the prayer *kapp* and did her best to fix her bun.

With one final look in the mirror, she left the room.

Janine waited next to the door. "Well, that's not so bad." The woman smiled as she gave her the once-over. "Noah's in the conference room waiting on you."

She followed the woman to the room.

"Here she is," Janine announced as they entered. Noah and Megan were talking quietly, and both turned as Rachel entered. The unreadable look in Noah's eyes made it hard to breathe normally.

She was aware of Janine watching the exchange and pulled her gaze from Noah. "*Denki* for the use of your clothes and the sneakers."

Janine patted her arm. "You're welcome." With one final look Noah's way, the woman left.

"I think I'll check in with Aden. See if he has news," Megan said, as if realizing Rachel and Noah had unfinished business between them.

Once they were alone, Noah pulled out a chair for Rachel.

He sat next to her and she waited for him to speak.

Noah gathered her hand in his. "I meant what I said earlier. I am sorry for the way things ended between us. My father realized we were getting serious. He told me you would be better off without me. You'd marry someone Amish like your parents wanted. I guess I believed him. I thought I was doing what was best for you." The bitterness in his tone was clear. "But we were friends and I should have stayed in touch, but it was just too hard. If I could change the past I would. But I want you to know what I felt for you was real, Rachel. I cared about you."

The sincerity in his eyes broke her heart. Why now? After all the years of wondering, thinking he'd left her because he didn't share her feelings, the truth was even harder to accept. Noah claimed to care about her, but he hadn't stood up to his father for her. Holding back tears was hard with her heart breaking again. She'd loved him with everything inside her and he'd left. Why hadn't Noah fought for them?

* * *

The vulnerability on her face condemned him. She was so beautiful and he'd often wondered what their future might have been if he hadn't let his father convince him leaving was the best thing for Rachel. All his dad really cared about was getting Noah away from her.

She glanced down at their joined hands. Seconds ticked by before she answered. "*Gott* had different plans for our lives," she said, her voice a shaky whisper. "What happened was for His purpose."

Though her answer wasn't unexpected, it still stung. What had he thought she'd say? The Amish believed things happened by God's will. Had Olivia's death been part of God's plan? Cynicism rose once more. Olivia was an innocent victim. Noah had been trying to get even with his father, and all he'd done was cost Olivia her life. Since her death, he'd tried his best to make amends. Joining the Lincoln County Sheriff's Department seemed like his calling for a while, but lately, he found himself longing for the less complicated way of life he'd had when he was with Rachel.

"Why didn't you tell me you were married?" she asked, her question taking him by surprise.

"Who told you?" he asked without answering right away.

"Theresa."

His mouth twisted in a bitter smile and he cleared his throat. "I don't know. I guess…" He stopped, not sure what he'd wanted to say. "We were only married for a short time. She died in a car accident."

The familiar pity he'd come to expect whenever he mentioned Olivia's death appeared on her face.

"I'm sorry, Noah, I didn't know. It is hard to lose someone you love."

He felt like a fake. Rachel cared for her husband. Olivia had been a means to get a rise out of his father.

Coming up with an answer was impossible. Noah was grateful to be spared the need when voices carried down the hall. Seconds later, Walker came in.

He could tell from Walker's drawn expression how difficult the evening had been for his mentor.

"Did anything useful turn up?" Noah asked without much hope.

The sheriff shook his head. "Not so far. Ryan is meeting Aden and the crime scene unit over at the house. I sent Theresa to her brother's place outside of Eureka. She's going to stay with him and his wife for a while until we can figure out what we're doing with the house."

Walker was a strong Christian man who had taught Noah what it meant to live in faith. He and Theresa would get through this, but Noah couldn't conceive of how hard it must have been to see the home in which they'd raised their two kids destroyed.

"Many of the men from the Amish community showed up to help out," Walker said to Rachel. Noah wasn't surprised. The Amish were all about helping those in need. He'd seen this acted out many times in his youth.

Janine came into the room and motioned to Walker and Noah.

They stepped out into the hall.

"What's going on?" Walker asked.

A grim line formed around Janine's mouth, warning bad news was to follow. "I took a call from a man who came off the Lake Koocanusa Bridge near Rexford. He stopped there to take a break." She hesitated. "Sheriff, the man is convinced he saw a body lying at the edge of the water."

Nothing could have prepared Noah for hearing this. "Is it a woman?" he asked, fearing the worst. Eva.

"The man wasn't sure, and he was too scared to get too close and it's dark. He said he could barely make it out as human."

"I'll get Megan and head over there," Walker said. "Call Cole and have him meet us. We'll need an ambulance and the coroner."

"You got it, Sheriff." Janine hurried off.

"Dear God, please don't let it be Eva," Walker prayed aloud.

Drawing in a deep breath, Walker said, "If it is Eva, they have whatever they were after and won't need to keep Rachel alive any longer, either."

The implication was frightening. Noah blew out a breath. "Rachel's going to want to come to the scene. In case it's Eva."

Walker glanced into the room at Rachel. "Let's hope that isn't the case." After a moment, he patted Noah's arm. "Watch out for her, Noah. I'll see you there," he said and left Noah to the task.

Blowing out a breath, he returned to the room.

Rachel looked up from pacing. "Something's happened." She saw what he could not hide. "Is it Eva?"

Noah wished that he could reassure her differently. "We don't know. Someone spotted a body near the water's edge on Lake Koocanusa."

Her hand flew to cover her mouth. "Oh no."

He held her arms and forced her to look at him. "We don't know anything yet."

"I want to go there. Noah, I have to see. If it's Eva, I want to be there for her."

After everything that happened, taking her out in public was dangerous, but he understood why she wanted to go, and half of the Lincoln County Sheriff's Department would be there. He prayed it would be enough.

Dread enhanced the faint lines on her face. "What if it is Eva? What am I going to do?"

He drew her into his arms. "We'll face it together. You're not alone."

When she pulled away, he let her go.

Noah cleared his throat. "If you're ready, we should go." All the old feelings from his youth rose to the surface. Letting them go was hard, but he'd hurt her enough already. He wouldn't hurt her again.

With Rachel next to him, he stopped at Janine's desk to let her know they'd be leaving.

Not answering, Janine stared out the window, a worried frown on her face. Very little rattled the woman.

He quickly whirled to the window. "Do you see something?" he asked. Noah squinted through the darkness, the streetlights barely providing enough light with the snow flurries.

"There's someone out there. I saw a man near your car."

The sheriff and Megan had already left. Aden and Ryan were at Walker's house. Cole was en route to the lake. Noah was on his own. "Lock the door. Stay here, and both of you get out of sight. I'm going to take a look around."

Rachel clutched his arm. "Noah, you can't go out there. It could be them."

"I'll be okay," he sought to reassure her, though he wasn't nearly as confident as his words suggested. "Make sure both doors are locked and stay out of sight."

Janine nodded. "Be careful, Noah. Whoever these men are, they've been watching the station. They probably know it's just you here."

He slowly opened the door and waited while Janine secured it behind him. As he peered through the falling snow, he noticed footprints—more than one set. Drawing his weapon, he eased toward the car.

The back tire on the passenger side was flat. Goose bumps popped up on his arms. Noah slipped around to the rear. Before he had time to react, a man dressed in black, his face obscured by a ski mask, jumped out from behind the vehicle.

A second man ran to the door of the sheriff's station. When he realized it was locked, he slammed his fist against the glass before running around the side of the building. He was going to try the rear door. Noah prayed Janine had time to lock it.

The first man lunged for Noah, slamming into him full force. They stumbled backward, hitting the ground hard. Noah's head bounced off the pavement, pain spreading from the contact point. The handgun slid on the snowy road out of his reach.

The man landed on top of him, a gun in his hand. He tried to position the weapon to fire at Noah's chest, but Noah seized the man's arm. With all his strength, he managed to twist the hand holding the gun to the ground and pounded it against the pavement while the man yelled for his buddy, his dark eyes filled with anger.

In the distance, Noah caught the noise of sirens. Help was on the way.

While he continued to try to wrestle the gun from the man's hand, the second man rounded the corner.

"Let's get out of here. There's more coming." Before Noah had time to think, the man on top of him slugged him hard with the butt of the weapon. Weight lifted from his body. Freed, Noah struggled to his knees. Through blurred visions he saw the two men running down the street away from the approaching patrol vehicle. Noah tried to get his feet under him. His stomach heaved. Inky blackness closed in. His last coherent thought was for Rachel. He'd failed her. He'd let them get away.

THIRTEEN

"Stay here. Noah's hurt." Janine ran from the station. Rachel didn't listen. Noah was in trouble because of her. Outside, the storm had regathered its strength and the wind renewed its fury. Red-and-blue lights bounced off the snowy world.

"Oh no." The words slipped out when Rachel spotted Noah lying on the cold ground. He wasn't moving. She ran to his side and knelt close. "Noah, are you okay?"

He didn't answer. She shook him gently, and he groaned.

"He needs medical help," Janine said, spotting the knot rising on the side of his temple. She ran for the approaching patrol car.

Noah still hadn't opened his eyes. "Noah, you have to wake up." Rachel couldn't bear the thought of something happening to him. In spite of their past, she would always care for him.

His eyes slowly fluttered open. He stared up at Rachel, and it was the best sight ever.

Two deputies reached them. Aden knelt by his friend. "Try not to move. Help is on its way."

Noah held a hand to his injured head and winced. "I'm okay." Slowly, he sat up, closing his eyes for a second.

"What happened?" Aden asked. "Ryan and I were on our way here when Janine called. She said two men were attacking you."

It took a moment for Noah to speak. "Janine saw some-one near my car, so I investigated. They slashed the pas-senger tire. As I circled it, one of the men jumped me."

Aden glanced up at the falling snow. "Let's get you inside and out of this." Aden lifted Noah to his feet and led him into the station.

Ryan returned a few minutes later. "It looks as if they had a car stashed around the corner. The footprints led me there. They appear to be heading out of town."

"The Ambo should be here soon. You need to let them take a look at your head," Janine insisted as she hovered over him like a mother hen.

Noah nodded, searching for Rachel amongst the group.

"Has there been any news from Walker?" he asked. With everything that happened, Rachel had almost for-gotten about the body.

"No. The weather's making the trip there difficult. I'll head over and assist," Ryan said. "Take care of yourself."

Noah lifted his hand as the deputy left the building.

Minutes later, the ambulance pulled up out front, and two paramedics came into the building.

While they examined Noah, Rachel stood watch next to Janine. All she could think about was that Noah could have died, and they were no closer to understanding why. More than ever she wished she had her *mamm* here with her. Beth had a way of helping Rachel find hope in even the worst of situations, including losing Daniel. She would give anything to possess *Mamm*'s strength, because it felt as if she were slowly unraveling inside.

Noah's stomach churned. His vision was less than clear. And he was terrified they'd find out Eva was dead.

He had to find someplace safe for Rachel to stay. Other

than his teammates, there was only one person he trusted to help him protect Rachel. His friend Isaac.

Isaac had built his home a little ways from his parents' place on the same land. He'd started out working as a carpenter for his father and uncle. Now, he ran his own crew of men. Because Isaac did work for both Amish and *Englischers*, his *daed* had approved him having a business phone.

When he was able to get a moment alone, Noah would call Isaac and ask for his help.

Next to him, Rachel cupped her coffee, her hands less than steady. Even though she'd been through so much, her beauty remained undeniable, as did his feelings for her. Noah shut down that train of thought. Rachel deserved better than him. He'd hurt her. And Olivia. He couldn't put Rachel through that again.

He shifted slightly and faced her. Even the tiniest of movements made him aware he hadn't quite returned to his normal self. "You look exhausted," he said. "There's a sofa in Walker's office. You should try and get some sleep."

She shook her head. "I can't think about sleep now. Not until I find out if…" She couldn't finish.

The fear in her eyes was clear.

He brushed his thumb across her cheek. She dropped her gaze, a soft sigh escaping.

"Rachel." There were so many things he wanted to say to her. Things that needed saying. Yet he couldn't voice a single one. Aden came into the room and stopped short at witnessing the intimate moment.

"Sorry to interrupt, but I have news."

Rachel rose to her feet. "Is it…?"

Aden shook his head. "It isn't your sister. The victim is male, around fifty-five to sixty in age."

Thank You, Lord. The prayer sped through Noah's head.

Please be with the man's family. As grateful as he was that it wasn't Eva, a family had lost someone they loved.

"Do we have any idea about the man's identity?" he asked.

Aden shook his head. "He didn't have any ID on him. Walker said there were skid marks on the road. It appears the man may have slid off the road and into the lake. The bridge was icy. It's looking like he may have gotten free of the car and tried to swim to shore, but the water's freezing. He probably died from hypothermia and his body washed ashore."

"So there's a good chance it was an accident," Noah said, surprised by the findings.

"I'm guessing as much. The coroner's there now. He'll take the man to the morgue and do an exam. Walker had him fingerprinted. Hopefully, we can identify him by his prints. Otherwise, we can take photos and try to see if anyone knows him. Chances are his car is at the bottom of the lake."

As tragic as it was, Noah had hoped this would lead to answers. Time was running out for Eva, and they had no idea why someone was coming after Rachel so aggressively.

Once Aden left, Rachel sank to her chair. "I am so grateful it wasn't Eva. Is that wrong? Someone died, and all I can think about is how happy I am it wasn't my sister."

Noah shook his head. "There's nothing wrong with being happy Eva isn't the one deceased. I feel the same way. It's natural."

She smiled at his response. "As hard as I try, I can't think of anything that will help us find her. I don't know why these men are coming after us, or who this man is she was seeing." She shrugged her helplessness.

"I'm guessing they have Eva stashed somewhere out of sight. But she's alive, Rachel. I firmly believe that."

Her smile widened, and he struggled to keep his reaction to himself. When she smiled like that, it reminded him of that sweet young girl who'd stolen his heart. Being around her again made him wish for so many things. He stumbled to his feet.

"I need to make a call," he said. She stared up at him confused. "Hang tight. I'll be right back." Noah left her without another word. Once he reached Walker's office, he closed the door and let the breath seep from his body. Foolish thoughts, and ones he'd best put out of his mind.

He pulled out his cell phone and called Isaac's business. When there was no answer, he glanced at his watch. Past five in the morning. While daylight was a little way out still, most of the Amish rose early. Isaac would no doubt be taking care of the chores around the homestead. Noah left a message but didn't go back right away. He needed a minute. Being close to Rachel again reminded him of all the things his younger self had wanted for his life. At the time, he hadn't given much thought to joining the Amish. He saw the difference between how his family interacted and the way the Amish treated each other, and he knew he wanted the Amish faith in his own life.

Noah dropped to the sofa, his head in his hands, confusion warring with what he thought he knew about himself. For so long, he'd tried to convince himself this job fulfilled him, as it gave him a chance to help others. But lately the work he did was no longer fulfilling. The sense of community he'd found among the Amish, their ability to forgive those who wronged them, well…more and more lately he longed for those things in his own life.

Foolish wishes. His life was here. This was his job, and he had plenty of things to make amends for.

FOURTEEN

Seated beside Noah in his patrol, the damaged tire changed, Rachel gazed out the window as they drove through the side streets of Eagle's Nest. In spite of the sweater Janine lent her, Rachel could not stop shaking. Noticing, Noah cranked the heat up another notch. In the filmy daylight of another day dawning, a fresh foot of snow covered the countryside.

"I spoke with Isaac, who talked to his dad. Bishop Aaron is pleased to have us stay with him and his wife." He glanced her way. "Isaac will be there, too."

He was trying to put her at ease, but Rachel hadn't felt safe since she'd woken up to find a stranger in her home.

The side mirror showed the empty street behind them. No strange car followed. Still, she couldn't relax.

Noah turned off the main highway and crossed the Silver Creek Bridge, which served as an unofficial boundary separating the Amish community from the rest of the county. If it weren't for what had happened, the beauty of the perfect world around her would be breathtaking. This morning, the mountains were almost completely obscured by low-hanging clouds indicating more snow was on the way.

Noah exited onto the Yoders' drive and slowed as he eased along the way.

Pulling in front of the house, he killed the engine and faced her. "Ready?"

She wasn't. Putting Bishop Aaron and his family in danger was the last thing she wanted.

Noah sensed her reluctance. "They'll be well protected. Cole and Ryan will be stationed around the property later today."

She drew in a breath. "I can't help but feel as if I should have some idea why this is happening."

"You had no way of predicting this outcome, Rachel." He held her gaze for a long moment. "Come on. Let's get you inside where it's warm."

Bishop Aaron must have heard the car pull up because he and his wife, Sadie, both came out to greet them on the porch.

"Welcome to our home. Please come in." Bishop Aaron waved his hand toward the door.

Inside, the warmth of the house slowly eased the chill from Rachel's body.

"We were getting ready to have breakfast," Sadie told them. "*Komm*, join us."

Sadie had the table set and ready for them.

"Isaac should be here soon. He helped me out with the morning chores. *Ach*, there he is." Bishop Aaron glanced out the rear door where Isaac stomped snow from his feet before coming inside. A smile lit his face when he saw Noah.

"It is *gut* to see you, my friend." Isaac gave Noah a hug.

"You, too, Isaac. I'm sorry it has to be under these circumstances."

Isaac's smile disappeared and he pivoted to Rachel. "I cannot believe such a thing is happening to you and Eva."

Rachel was glad he and Noah stayed in touch. *"Denki,"* she murmured.

"Sit, everyone. We must eat while the food is warm," Sadie urged.

Rachel claimed the chair Sadie indicated while Noah sat next to her.

Once the table quieted, Bishop Aaron lowered his head in preparation for the silent prayer. Rachel folded her hands in her lap. So many things pressed in on her, but *Gott* knew her heart when there were no words.

When Bishop Aaron said, "Amen," she slowly lifted her head. Beside her, Noah stared at his plate, a single muscle working in his jaw giving away his soul's disquiet. She wondered what he'd prayed for.

Though the food was delicious, Rachel ate very little. Thoughts of her sister's well-being took away her appetite. She was grateful for the conversation between Noah and Isaac. It helped to draw her attention from her concerns.

When the meal finished, Rachel helped Sadie clear away the table, then wash the dishes.

It felt as if this exhaustion growing inside her bore down to her soul. She wanted to this nightmare to end. Wanted Eva home safely.

"Noah will do everything he can to find Eva," Sadie assured her, as if reading her thoughts.

Rachel shifted to find the kind woman watching her. "I know, but I am worried about my *schweschder*. It has been days without any word."

Sadie placed a hand on her arm. "*Gott* will take care of Eva, I know it."

Rachel so wanted to believe. She nodded. "*Jah, Gott* will take care of her."

"I made up a room for you. It belonged to my Faith. You know she married a few years ago and moved away. I miss her terribly," Sadie said, a watery smile on her face. "But she and her *mann* will be coming home for Christmas in a month's time. I received a letter from her. She has a surprise for me. I think she is with child."

Rachel's smile slipped. No one but her mother and Eva knew about the baby she'd lost. The possible barrenness that resulted from the accident. Even though a year had passed, the pain followed her each day.

"That is *gut* news," she forced out, happy for Sadie's blessing.

Sadie beamed. "*Ach*, and I have a dress that once belonged to Faith along with one of her prayer coverings. You and she are close to the same size."

Sadie showed her to the room and opened the chest at the foot of the bed. Pulling out a dark blue dress and white prayer *kapp*, she held them up for Rachel.

"I know you are in your mourning period, but I am sure it will be *oke*."

Rachel took the garments from her. *"Denki."*

"You look tired, *kinna*. Why don't you try to get some rest? Things will appear much better once you've slept."

Sadie moved to the door and touched the handle. "And when you are awake, I will make us some *kaffe* and apple fry pies. You hardly touched your breakfast. You must keep your strength up, Rachel. For yourself and for Eva."

Stepping across the threshold, Sadie quietly closed the door. For the first time since she woke up to find a stranger in her home, Rachel sank to the bed and wept.

"It's a surprise to see you and Rachel together again," Isaac said, as direct as always. He stirred the fire in the stove, then pivoted in time to catch Noah's reaction.

Isaac was one of the few people Noah had ever shared his true feelings for Rachel with.

"It's my job." Noah tried to downplay the situation.

Isaac agreed with a nod. *"Jah*, but I see the way you look at her. You still have feelings for her."

As much as Noah wished to deny the truth, he couldn't.

"Well, it doesn't matter. You know I'm no good at relationships."

"I know you are too hard on yourself," Isaac said instead of agreeing with Noah.

"I have a job to do, and when that's finished, when Eva is home safely, I will return to my life and Rachel will return to hers. I'm not Amish, Isaac."

"But you wish to be. Always have, admit it. Who knows what might have happened if you had been allowed to follow your heart."

Noah had to put an end to the direction of their conversation. It served no purpose. "Things turned out the way they were intended. Rachel married. I became a deputy. All's well."

Before Isaac could respond, Bishop Aaron came into the room. His gaze shot from his son to Noah as if sensing the tension.

"I must make my rounds. Many people are sick in the community. I will keep you and Rachel in my prayers."

Noah was grateful for the bishop's timely interference. "Thank you," he murmured.

After the bishop left, Noah was saved from continuing the conversation when his phone rang.

"I need to take this," he told Isaac.

His friend nodded. "I must be on my way. I have orders to fill. I'll speak with you later." Isaac grabbed his coat and hat and headed outside while Noah answered the call.

"We may have something," Cole's excited tone came through the phone crystal clear.

"That's great," Noah said, and under his breath, he murmured, "Thank You, God."

"The news of Eva's disappearance has spread through the Amish community, and a couple stopped in a little while ago. It seems they were returning home on the night

Eva disappeared and saw a vehicle on the side of the road. As they passed, they noticed a couple of men in the large SUV. They were pretty sure there was a woman in the back. It could have been Eva."

Relief and shock warred for control. "They didn't happen to get a license plate number?" Noah was sure he already knew the answer. The couple wouldn't be looking for anything sinister. Staring out the window, he watched as Isaac headed the buggy down the lane to the road.

"No, but they're pretty sure they saw some advertising sign on the side of the vehicle. Unfortunately, they couldn't make out what it said."

Noah's hope evaporated. "So we don't have anything solid." He stepped outside. The clean mountain air filled his lungs. Leaving the porch, Noah glanced around the property. An uneasy feeling robbed him of the ability to relax. He moved to the side of the house where the woods encroached and peered into them. Nothing moved. Was his reaction due to what they'd gone through?

"We have a description of the vehicle. It's something. The couple said it was too dark to make out anything about the men." Cole stopped, waiting for Noah's response.

"Stay positive," Cole said, reading his thoughts. "We're going to get these guys. I know we are."

Noah prayed they would, but he couldn't be more discouraged. "Any progress on identifying the man in the lake?" he asked instead.

"Nope. His prints aren't in the system. We're passing out flyers to see if anyone around town knew him. I sure hope we can identify him to give his family some peace of mind. How are you feeling? That was some blow you took."

His head still hurt like crazy. "I'm okay." A door creaked behind him, and he spun around. Rachel came down the steps to where he stood.

"I'll keep you posted on identifying the vehicle. As soon as we have anything, I'll give you a call. Ryan is heading your way soon."

"Good. Thanks, Cole." Noah ended the call and put the phone away.

Rachel stopped beside him, her worried eyes scanned his face. "Has something happened?"

The last thing he wanted was to get her hopes up, but he couldn't keep this from her. He told her about the SUV.

Relief softened some of the tautness from her face. "This is *gut*. If we can identify who owns the SUV, we can find Eva."

"Yes, but it was dark, and the couple didn't pay that much attention to the vehicle."

Her expression fell, and he felt like a heel. She needed something to keep her going.

"I'm sorry. I don't mean to sound discouraging. It's something."

Noah stared at the mountains in the distance. The beauty of the snow-covered peaks always had the power to ground him.

The skies had cleared with the afternoon, though the chill remained. He noticed Rachel wrapped her sweater closer around her body.

"We should head back inside. It's not safe out here in the open like this." As they started toward the home, the noise of a vehicle approaching on the main road had him whirling on alert. It was too soon for it to be Ryan.

"Hurry," he said and clutched her elbow, urging her toward the house. As they reached the side, the door opened. A masked man stepped out onto the porch. His heart slammed into his chest. *Sadie.*

Noah tugged Rachel out of sight, torn between protecting her and ensuring Sadie's well-being. He pointed to the woods behind them. "We need to get out of sight," he whispered. They ran for cover. Tucking behind a tree, Noah watched the man in the mask leave the porch. He stared down the lane as the vehicle noise drew closer. A dark brown SUV eased down the lane. Its windows were tinted dark, making it impossible to see inside. It appeared as if at one time, a company logo had adorned the door like the couple indicated, but someone had removed it recently.

The man in the mask moved toward the vehicle. The driver slowed as he reached the front of the house. When the masked man got inside, Noah caught a glimpse of the driver.

"He's not wearing a mask," Rachel exclaimed. Noah couldn't believe it either. He got a good look at the driver's face in those seconds before the door closed and committed it to memory. After what felt like forever, the SUV slowly turned around. They were leaving.

Noah grabbed his phone and called Ryan. "Where are you?" he asked as soon as Ryan answered.

"I'm about fifteen minutes out. Is everything okay?"

"No, they found us." He quickly explained what they faced.

"I'm on my way. I'll call in Cole to assist. Stay safe." Noah ended the call without answering.

"Ryan's close," he said to ease Rachel's fears. "Let's get back inside as fast as we can. I'm worried about Sadie."

As they moved through the woods, the SUV suddenly braked a little way down. Noah stopped and watched. The vehicle backed up.

Noah tucked Rachel close. The SUV eased backward.

It reached the house, then shifted toward the woods and stopped directly in front of them. They were trapped between the house and two very dangerous men who seemed to have nothing to lose.

FIFTEEN

The SUV continued to idle. Through the windshield, the driver appeared to be staring at something on the ground. Their footprints.

Noah slowly unholstered his weapon. Her heart accelerated at the sight of it.

"What if they come after us?" she whispered. The words barely left her mouth before both men climbed out.

Drawing her closer, Noah spoke against her ear, "Be as quiet as you can."

She kept her face buried against his chest. The noise of the men tromping through the snow seemed to reverberate all around them.

Time slowed to nothing while all sorts of terrible outcomes raced through her head. She was terrified for them. For Sadie. Noah's steady heartbeat against her ear kept her from losing it.

"Over there!" one of the men yelled. "I see them. Let's get her and get rid of him." She recognized the voice. He was the man who tried to kidnap her from her house.

Both men charged them.

"Get down." Noah pushed her to the ground, stepped from the tree coverage and opened fire.

Rachel covered her head with her hands as the men returned fire and the noise was deafening. Noah ducked behind the tree as several shots lodged inches from his head. It was two against one and she was terrified for Noah.

In the distance a siren screamed through the countryside. Help was on the way.

Noah waited for a lull in the shooting before returning fire.

When the men reciprocated, the shots sounded farther away.

"They're leaving. They must have heard the patrol car coming," Noah told her.

The engine roared. Tires squealed. "Stay here," Noah said and headed after the SUV, aiming for the tires.

Rachel jumped to her feet and moved from the tree coverage in time to see the SUV's driver hold something out of the open window. A gun.

"Noah!" she shouted.

Noah saw the weapon and took cover. The driver continued firing as the SUV flew down the lane and out of sight.

Noah ran back to her. "Let's go inside and check on Sadie." They headed across the yard and up the porch steps. Opening the door, Rachel stumbled across the threshold with Noah. He slid the lock into place.

"Sadie," Rachel called out before heading toward the kitchen.

"I'm in here." Sadie peeked out of her bedroom, her face drawn.

"Oh, thank You, Lord," Rachel said and hugged her tight. "We were so worried about you."

"I saw him coming from the window. I thought he would kill me, so I hid under the bed. I could hear him moving through the house, but he just left."

"He must have heard Noah and me talking. I'm just glad you're okay."

Noah moved to the window, taking out his phone. "I'm going to see if Ryan can cut these guys off before they get away." Rachel listened while Noah explained what happened.

"Those gunshots." A sigh lifted Sadie's shoulders. "I was so afraid they would harm you both. *Gott* protected you." With a shake of her head, she said, "I will put on some *kaffe* and heat the fry pies. I think we all could use something to take our minds off what is happening."

When she and Noah were alone, Rachel went over to him. "I thought he would kill you." Tears hovered in her eyes.

"But he didn't," he said softly. "I'm fine."

How many people would have to suffer because of these men's evil intentions? If something happened to Noah, she would not be able to forgive herself. In spite of what they'd gone through in the past, she cared about him. A part of her heart would always belong to Noah.

He whispered her name, his voice rough with some emotion she wished to understand. She ducked her head. Noah deserved happiness in his life. More than anything she wished she could be the one to make him happy, but he needed someone who was whole. Someone who could give him the family he deserved.

Cole pulled up out front and Noah turned to Rachel. "I'll be right back," he told her and stepped out onto the porch and waited until she'd slid the locks into place. Glancing around the tranquil setting, his heart was in chaos. She was always in his thoughts. His heart. Being close to her again reminded him that he wasn't over her. He doubted if he'd ever be over her.

Noah stepped off the porch and went over to Cole's cruiser.

"Anything?" The question proved unnecessary after Noah got a good look at Cole's expression.

"I just heard from Ryan. He drove past here and up the road for a bit. There was no sign of the vehicle."

Frustrated, Noah ran a hand through his hair. "Which means they probably live around here."

"Exactly. I have Stephanie running a check through DMV for Suburbans fitting the description you gave me. Maybe we'll get a hit."

"Let's hope so. Rachel and I got a good look at the SUV's driver. I'll take her to the station and see if either of us can pick him out of the mug books."

"That sounds like a good idea. Ryan's heading back here now. He's going to park at the edge of the lane near the road. We'll keep watch on the family in case these guys come back."

Noah was grateful for Cole's help. "Thanks. I don't think these men would harm the Yoders. Their only focus appears to be getting to Rachel. Still, I don't want to take any chances."

He glanced up at the house. For Rachel, he prayed for a happy ending, but nothing about what he'd seen so far led him to believe it would happen.

He stepped up on the porch and knocked. Rachel peeked through the window before opening the door.

"Did they catch them?" she asked.

He shook his head. "We should probably go to the station. If we can identify the driver, we can bring him in. Find out what he knows about Eva's disappearance."

Rachel nodded. "I'll let Sadie know."

Glancing out the window, Noah spotted Isaac's buggy heading their way.

When Rachel came back with Sadie, Noah turned from the window. "Isaac's home. I'll let him know what's happened before we leave. Will you do me a favor?" he asked Sadie, and the old woman nodded without hesitation. "Keep the doors locked. There will be a couple of patrol vehicles watching your home for a while, but I want to be sure you're safe."

He hated that he was responsible for the fear he saw in Sadie's eyes.

Noah waited while Rachel slipped on the sweater Janine had given her and hugged Sadie. "I pray for *Gott*'s protection on the both of you and Eva," Sadie told them.

"Denki," Rachel managed and waved as they left the house.

Outside, Noah had a brief word with Cole before he and Rachel went to the barn. Isaac glanced up from his task of unhitching the mare. "Are you leaving us?" he asked.

"We are." Noah explained what had happened earlier. "Please thank your father for allowing us to stay here, but it's best if we find another place else to hide. I don't want to put your family in any more danger."

"Where will you go?"

"We'll find someplace safe." He held out his hand. "Thank you, my friend."

Isaac clasped it. "You are both welcome here at any time. Be safe, Noah. I want you to be at my wedding. Don't go getting yourself hurt."

Noah smiled and waved at his friend. He and Rachel walked together to his truck. As he climbed behind the wheel, Noah couldn't get Isaac's parting words out of his head. With what they were facing now, Isaac's wedding felt light-years away.

SIXTEEN

Rachel expected to see the man in the SUV around every turn along the way. Her heart wouldn't slow down no matter how hard she tried to relax.

"You're safe," Noah told her when she glanced behind them for the second time.

She faced him. Noah was doing everything in his power to protect her.

He'd grown up from that boy she'd known so well. What might have been was there in the shadows of her mind, just out of reach.

Noah caught her watching him and reached for her hand, entwining their fingers. "Tell me about your husband?" he asked, the question taking her by surprise.

She pulled her hand free and focused her attention out the front window.

"He was a special man," she said quietly. "Daniel was shy, but once he knew you, you couldn't stop him from talking. And he loved farming. He and my *daed* spent long hours working the land, planting, harvesting. Daniel never complained. He loved everything about life."

"He sounds like a nice man," Noah murmured with a catch in his voice that made her curious.

"I think you would have liked him."

Noah's grip tightened on the wheel. "I'm sure. I heard

about the accident, but I wasn't on duty that day." She sensed it wasn't entirely true.

Talking about the moment when her life changed forever still hurt. "I'm still not sure what happened that day." She stopped. They'd been talking about the baby. Rachel hadn't been feeling well. The ride home had been uneventful until… "Something spooked the mare. She reared up, bolted. Daniel was thrown from the buggy right away. He hit his head on a rock. They said he suffered a brain hemorrhage." She shook her head. "He never woke up."

"I'm so sorry, Rachel." She could feel his eyes on her, yet the emotions clogging her throat prevented words. "You didn't deserve to lose your husband so young, and you certainly don't deserve what's happening now."

She drew in a needed breath, forced aside the pain. "What about you? I can't imagine how hard it was for you to lose your wife so young."

His jaw tightened. "It wasn't the same," he murmured. "What happened between Olivia and me was nothing like you and Daniel."

She didn't understand. "Why?"

His mouth twisted in a bitter smile. "I didn't love Olivia. In the beginning, I told myself I did, but I was just trying to get back at my father."

The look in his eye sent her pulse racing. "But you married her," she managed.

"Because I knew it would infuriate my dad. He hated that you and I were close and he did his best to keep us apart. When I started college, I met Olivia, and I convinced myself I cared about her, so we eloped. I couldn't wait to tell Dad we were married." He shook his head. "His reaction was everything I wanted. My father insisted we get the marriage annulled. We were too young to wed in his opinion, and he wanted me to finish school. Make something of myself. I refused. In his mind, it was just another act of rebellion on my part, and I guess he was right. We didn't speak for a long time." Noah flexed his hands on the wheel. "It didn't take long for both Olivia and me to realize we'd made a huge mistake. We fought all the time. We were both going to school and working full-time just to pay the bills. Olivia and I rarely saw each other, and when we did, we argued."

Her heart ached for him. She'd had no idea what Noah went through. "I am so sorry," she murmured, but he didn't seem to hear.

"Then, one night after we fought, Olivia left. Said it was for good." The bleakness in his eyes was hard to take. "I should have stopped her. The weather was awful, near blizzard conditions outside, but I let my anger consume me. The funny thing is, it had nothing to do with Olivia."

"What happened?" she asked, knowing how difficult it was for him to continue.

"She lost control of the car and plunged off the side of the mountain. She died instantly." He stopped. Focused straight ahead. "That's when I hit rock bottom. I knew if I didn't get help, I wouldn't make it."

With a lift of his shoulders, he said, "You know my family wasn't much on believing in God growing up. I ended up going to one of the churches in town with Walker and Theresa. It changed my life." He looked over at her. "I found God, and I knew He'd given me a second chance and I wasn't about to screw it up. When I graduated from college, I came home and joined the sheriff's department. In a way, I think God led me here." He paused for a moment. "I couldn't save Olivia, but what I'm doing now helps others. As hard as it was to let you go back then, I guess in a way I'm grateful I did. If I'd stayed and we married, the old me would have messed things up between us."

She broke eye contact. Through the years she'd always been curious about what might have been had Noah not moved away. Imagined what their life together might be like. Now she knew. It was just a foolish childhood dream.

Megan's voice came through the radio breaking the silence between them. "Dispatch, this is Deputy Clark requesting immediate backup at MT 37 south of Forest Road 92. I have a vehicle fitting the description reported by Deputy Warren on the side of the road. It appears abandoned."

Noah's gaze flew to Rachel. "That's close," she said.

"We're five minutes out, but I can't risk putting you in danger by responding. It could be a setup…"

"Megan may be in danger, Noah. You must help her."

With doubts crowding in, he eventually hit the radio on his shoulder. "Stephanie, this is Deputy Warren. I'm five minutes out, but I have Rachel with me. I can back Megan up until another deputy arrives on scene."

"10-4, Noah. Ryan is en route, as well. He'll be there soon. In the meantime, you stay safe," Stephanie said.

"10-4." Noah increased the truck's speed as much as he dared. Though the county had plowed the road recently, the new accumulation made the conditions hazardous.

Noah pulled off on MT 37. The Lake Koocanusa Bridge came into view. They were near the spot where the man's body had been discovered. As he glanced out at the lake, a niggling of doubt resurfaced. Most people around the county knew the hazards of crossing the bridge in winter conditions. If their John Doe had lived near here, he would have known of these dangers.

As he passed over the bridge, he spotted the sign for

the forest road. A little way beyond the turnoff, Megan's patrol car sat off the road, lights flashing.

Easing onto the shoulder, Megan exited the vehicle and headed his way. Noah did a quick survey of the area. He shifted in his seat.

Ryan pulled up behind them and Noah breathed a sigh of relief. "Ryan's here. I'll speak with them for a second before we leave."

He climbed out and she hit the locks. Noah went over to where Megan waited with Ryan.

"Aden's on his way, as well," Ryan said.

"Good. As soon as he arrives, I'll take Rachel to the station." He turned to Megan. "What do you have?"

"There was no one in the vehicle when I arrived. The engine's still warm, though, so they were here not too long ago. They made sure to take anything inside the vehicle that might incriminate them. I haven't searched the woods yet."

"Keep your radios close and your eyes open," Noah warned before returning to the truck. When Rachel unlocked the door, he slid inside.

"Aden's on his way to assist. As soon as he arrives, we'll go. I hate to leave them without backup."

"Do you think they are close?" She glanced out the side window.

Noah stared at the abandoned vehicle. Why had the men left it? Did they have engine trouble…or a plan?

"It's possible," he said, turning to her. "I won't let them hurt you, Rachel."

In the woods, he caught glimpses of Megan and Ryan as they searched. All the while, he couldn't shake the feeling there was something off about this whole situation.

The disturbing thought had barely cleared his head when a noise broke the silence. The crack of a gun firing.

The back window shattered. Noah pushed Rachel down low as a bullet whizzed past.

Shoving the cruiser in gear, Noah shot down the road, keeping as low as possible while still being able to see where he was going. More shots destroyed the driver's-side mirror. They were aiming for him.

He hit the radio. "Shots fired, shots fired." Noah filled them in on what had happened.

"We see them," Megan's strained voice came over the radio. "Freeze! Sheriff's department!"

Noah pulled to the side of the road and listened for updates while praying for his fellow deputies.

"I just arrived on the scene," Aden said. "I see Megan and Ryan. They're in pursuit. I'm going after them."

Noah punched the radio. "Be safe," he said and glanced over at Rachel. Terror filled her eyes. He pulled her into his arms.

"It's okay. We're safe."

She drew away and looked into his eyes. "It isn't. It isn't anything close to okay."

In the distance, an engine fired. Noah listened to what could be a four-wheeler, the driver pushing the machine to its limit as the sound faded. These men had planned this attack out very carefully, right down to stashing an escape vehicle in the woods.

Noah brushed a strand of fire-red hair from her face without answering.

These men had gone to great lengths to get to Rachel. That spoke of someone who had nothing to lose. They'd keep coming. And it would take everyone in the Lincoln County Sheriff's Department to keep Rachel alive long enough to find out what really happened to Eva.

SEVENTEEN

Rachel glanced up from searching through the mug book in front of her when Noah entered the conference room at the station. He handed her a cup of coffee. "I thought you could use a pick-me-up."

She smiled in spite of how hopeless she felt. *"Denki."*

"Any of them look familiar?" he asked and pointed to the book she'd been studying.

She shook her head. "I'm afraid not. How about you?"

He scraped his chair back and sat. "Same, but I'm willing to bet the driver has a criminal background. He somehow slipped up by not wearing his ski mask."

Rachel took a sip of coffee and watched him across the rim of her cup. "Did they find anything useful in the abandoned vehicle?" In her head, she ticked off the number of days since Eva had disappeared. Too many.

Noah shook his head and shifted in his chair. "No doubt he wore gloves, so we won't be able to lift any prints. The license plate on the vehicle was reported stolen. It belongs to a car out near Rexford. Ryan's heading there now to speak with the owners. See if they remember seeing anyone suspicious hanging around." He held her gaze and she tried not to give in to the panic growing inside her.

"She's been missing for too long, hasn't she?"

Noah gathered her hand in his. "Don't go there," he murmured.

She struggled to keep from falling apart, dropping her gaze to their joined hands. "I want to be strong, but it's hard." Rachel couldn't imagine what her *mamm*'s reaction would be when she returned to West Kootenai in a few days.

"Look at me," Noah said quietly, and she did. "There's a reason why they need you, and I don't for a minute believe they'll harm Eva until they have both of you. She's alive for now. That's all that matters because it buys us time. My team is working round the clock to bring her home safely. I need you to do your part and not give up hope."

She'd witnessed firsthand how hard Noah worked to protect her and find Eva. Looking at his handsome face, she touched his cheek. "I will, I promise."

He swallowed visibly and covered her hand with his. His dark eyes filled with something unknown.

She felt as if she were drowning in them.

She stumbled to her feet and turned away. She couldn't go there with him again. It hurt too much.

"I'm sorry," he murmured, his voice unsteady.

She drew in a breath and struggled for a calm that would not come.

The door opened. Both she and Noah turned. She was grateful for the interruption.

"Noah, can I speak with you for a moment?" the sheriff asked. Rachel could not imagine how things must appear to him.

"Sure. I'll be right back," Noah told her. She didn't look at him as he left the room.

The door closed softly, and she let go of the breath she'd been holding inside. No matter how hard she tried, she couldn't deny having feelings for Noah still. He was her first love, but she wasn't that young girl anymore, and she must not let her heart get tangled up in the past again.

Instinctively, Rachel touched her stomach, the pain of what she'd lost with her always. Her child. Her precious baby, gone. All hopes of a happy future had disappeared with the babe.

After the accident, Rachel hadn't thought she'd make it through the sorrow without falling apart. She wouldn't have, without Eva and her *mamm*. The funeral had been a somber time. Watching as her husband's casket was lowered into the frozen ground had been like a knife to her heart.

In the days that followed, she tried to pick up the pieces of her life, wanted to be strong for Beth and Eva because she knew they worried about her. Yet each time she saw a family together, it reminded her of all the things that would never be hers.

She'd pored through the Bible during those days, finding comfort in a favorite scripture.

Finally, my brethren, be strong in the Lord, and in the power of his might. Put on the whole armour of God, that ye may be able to stand against the wiles of the devil.

Behind her, the door opened. Rachel slowly turned. Noah held something in his hand, and her attention was drawn to it as horror coursed down her limbs.

"Where did you get that?" she asked.

Noah came to her. "We found it stuffed under the back seat of the SUV. You recognize it?" He held up the evidence bag.

Her hand covered her trembling mouth. "It's Eva's cloak. She wore it the day she disappeared."

Rachel took it from him and clutched the evidence bag

tight. Her sister was out there somewhere, cold and all alone, and Rachel had no idea how to help Eva.

"We're searching all the cabins around the lake area. If he has her hidden there, we'll find her," Noah said. Rachel didn't respond. She hadn't slept in days. Rest would do a world of good, but more than anything she needed answers.

"Why don't I get you some food?" he said, but she shook her head.

"I don't think I can eat anything."

Noah laid the evidence bag on the table. "You need to try. I'll have Stephanie run to the diner and get something. Why don't you keep looking at the photos?"

"Do you mind if we go to the restaurant ourselves?" she asked instead. "I could use some fresh air. I feel as if the walls are closing in, and all I can think about is Eva."

Even though the last thing he needed was to be taking her out in public again, he understood how she felt.

"I'll check in with Walker, but I'm sure it'll be okay." He pressed her hand and let her go. He stepped out in the hall and ran a hand across his eyes. He wanted to bring Eva home for Rachel's sake, but so far it felt like an impossible wish.

The last time he'd seen Walker, the sheriff had been about to try to get some sleep himself. Now, Noah spotted him talking on the phone. Apparently sleep hadn't been an option.

Noah waited until he'd finished speaking. The expression on Walker's face was disturbing.

"Anything wrong?" Noah asked, not sure he was ready for more bad news.

"That was Megan. They've searched all of the cabins

in the area. There's no sign of Eva." Walker blew out a breath. "I don't like it, Noah. Too much time has passed."

Seeing the concern from the man who personified strength reminded Noah of how crucial it was to find Eva soon.

Walker shook off his misgiving. "Did Rachel recognize the cloak?"

"She did. It's Eva's. It appears Eva was in that vehicle at some point."

"And there are lots of roads leading out of town. They could be anywhere."

"Rachel and I will keep looking at the books. I'm praying this guy is in there somewhere."

"Me, too," Walker said. "Because we sure could use a break."

Noah shared Walker's sentiments. "I'm going to take Rachel across the street to get something to eat. She could use a break and some fresh air. I know it's not ideal, but we won't be long."

Walker nodded. "Be careful. These guys are ruthless."

With Walker's warning still ringing in his ears, Noah returned to Rachel. "We're good to go. Are you ready?"

She nodded and stepped from the room beside him.

Shoving his arms in his jacket, he opened the door and glanced around at the mild foot traffic around town. Noah searched the faces of the few men milling about, relieved the man in the SUV wasn't among them.

With Noah keeping Rachel tucked to the inside of the sidewalk, they reached the crosswalk. He punched the Walk button. Once the light changed, he took Rachel's hand, and they headed across the street. Out of the corner of his eye, he noticed a vehicle pull out onto the road. The hairs on the back of his neck rose as he whirled toward the sound. Though the light was red, the car showed no signs of slowing. Noah had just enough time to push Rachel out of the way before the car slammed into him. His left knee hit the bumper. He bounced onto the hood, striking his shoulder on the windshield before landing on the pavement where his head hit, hard.

Pain strobed from the contact points on his leg and shoulder. Head. Two men jumped out of the vehicle. Both were armed.

"Stay down," he yelled to Rachel and yanked his Glock from its holster.

The masked driver opened fire on Noah. Bullets whizzed past his head, and he tucked as close to the ground as possible. They were trying to keep him incapacitated while they went after Rachel.

"Noah!" Rachel screamed. He swiveled in time to see the terror on her face as a second man in a ski mask rushed toward her.

"Get the girl!" the driver shouted. With what little strength Noah could muster, he rolled onto his side and fired at the driver advancing on him, striking the man in the chest. The man dropped to the ground. Flipping to the second man, Noah shot again, and the gunman fell to the ground.

All Noah could think about was Rachel. He stumbled to his feet. The world spun and his stomach heaved. "Hurry, Rachel, there might be more." She scrambled up next to him and put her arm around his waist for support.

"We have to get to the station." Trying to put one foot in front of the other became an impossible struggle. His leg hurt like crazy, and he was pretty sure he'd dislocated his shoulder. From where they stood, the station might as well be on the other side of the moon. Yet he had to try. Both attackers might still be alive.

Staying lucid was a struggle, and he fought to keep

from losing consciousness. Putting one foot in front of the other, he focused on the sidewalk. If they could reach it…

His vision became fuzzy and he stumbled, landing hard against Rachel, his weight took them both down onto the pavement.

"Noah!" She cradled him close. Nearby, tires screeched. Voices drifted through the fog, and his fear accelerated. Did the shooter call for backup?

"Go to the station. Get help." He thought he said the words aloud, but he was fading fast. *Hurry, Rachel.* The thought raced through his mind.

"Noah! Hang on. Help is coming. Please don't leave me." Her words floated above him like clouds, the panic evident even in his haze. She was worried about him. And he still cared for her.

"I wish things were different," he murmured. *Wish I could be the man you need.* Unsure if he'd said it aloud, he prayed he hadn't. He'd hurt her enough. She needed his protection, not his useless wishes. *You need someone who can love you and be strong for you.* The words appeared in his head. Was he having the conversation with her? Not at all.

Objects crowded in, too blurred to make out. Noah closed his eyes. He hurt everywhere. Someone screamed his name. Regret brought a tear to his eye. Rachel. *I'm sorry.* He thought he'd said it aloud but was too tired to know. *I'm just sorry I hurt you.*

EIGHTEEN

"Please, somebody!" Rachel screamed. Cradling Noah's upper body in her lap, she glanced frantically around, tears streaming down her cheeks. "Somebody help us!"

Noah mumbled something unintelligible. Someone pulled her away.

"No!" She fought her restrainer.

"I need you to come with me," Walker urged, while holding her arms. "You could still be in danger."

"I'm staying with Noah." Noah had risked his life to save her. She wouldn't leave him now.

The world around her became a whirl of activity. An ambulance rolled up next to where Noah had now begun to waken. EMTs rushed to assist while Aden and Megan hurried to the two men who lay still on the pavement.

Noah slowly sat up even though the EMTs urged him to remain still. He glanced around. When his eyes found hers, she pulled free of Walker and hurried to his side.

"Are you okay?" he asked, clutching her hand, his voice barely audible.

"I am fine." She held on to his hand while one of the EMTs examined his shoulder and the second cut his pants away from the injured leg. Noah winced in pain as the EMT made sure there were no broken bones.

I wish things were different. Wish I could be the man

you need... Remembering the words he'd mumbled broke her heart.

"There are no broken bones, but your knee has begun swelling. You need to stay off it for a while and keep it iced," the female EMT told him, then glanced at her partner.

"Shoulder's dislocated," her partner said. "You could have injured your head when you hit the ground. You already have a concussion. We need to get you to the hospital."

Noah shook his head. "No hospital," he told the male EMT. "Do what you have to do here."

"It's going to hurt like crazy," the man warned.

"I'll be okay. Just do it," Noah said, his voice barely audible.

The EMT's opinion was clear, but he did as Noah asked.

Easing Noah onto his back, with his injured arm away from his body at a ninety-degree angle, he grasped his wrist and positioned a foot against Noah's waist.

"Ready?" he asked Noah.

Noah nodded and kept his eyes on Rachel.

The EMT pulled Noah's arm hard. Noah clamped down on his bottom lip as the shoulder slipped back into its socket.

"You'll need to keep it immobile for a while," the EMT informed him while his partner returned with a sling and placed it around Noah's neck, gently easing his arm into place.

"Can you help me up?" Noah asked the sheriff. Placing his arms around Noah's waist, Walker brought him up to his feet.

"Noah, you need to sit down," Rachel said. He appeared so weak.

"I'm okay." Though his voice sounded strained, he managed a smile. He glanced behind them at the two men lying on the ground. Their faces uncovered.

"They're both dead," Walker told him. "If you hadn't shot them, they would have killed you and taken Rachel."

"Any ID?" Noah asked when Aden stopped next to them.

He shook his head. "None in the car, either. I've printed both of them. Hopefully, they're in the system. Did either of you recognize them as the man from the SUV?"

"I've never seen either of them. Have you?" Noah asked Rachel.

She shook her head. How many people were involved in this plot?

"There's the coroner." Walker nodded toward an older man in a suit coming their way. Walker introduced Doctor Jenkins to Rachel before turning to Noah. "You need to go to the station and lie down for a while. Otherwise, I'm ordering Aden to take you to the hospital right now."

Noah managed a smile. "Yes, sir."

"I'll go with you," Aden said. "I'm anxious to see if either of these men's prints are in the system. Can you make it on your own?"

"I think so," Noah said.

Rachel stuck close as they slowly reached the station.

Janine met them at the door. "Oh, dear. I just came on duty and I hear you've been hurt."

Though he tried to pretend differently, Rachel could see him fading fast.

"I'm okay, but I think I'll lie down for a bit. Can you keep an eye out for Rachel?"

"Don't worry about Rachel. She's in good hands. Go rest. I'll bring you some ice for that leg."

"I'll go run these prints." Aden held up the fingerprint cards. "As soon as I have anything, I'll come get you."

Noah nodded, slowly easing down the hall, the swelling in his leg making each step a struggle.

As Rachel watched him disappear, she couldn't believe how close to dying he'd come.

"He's going to be fine," Janine said. "Noah is tough as nails." The woman placed her arm around Rachel's shoulders. "Stephanie said you and Noah were on your way to get something to eat. Why don't I order pizza from down the street and you can keep me and Stephanie company until it arrives?"

They reached the dispatch station. Stephanie glanced up from manning the phones. "Calls have been pouring in. Such a frightening thing to happen, and outside the station no less."

Janine pulled up an extra chair for Rachel and slipped into the seat next to Stephanie.

With the food ordered, Stephanie excused herself to assist the sheriff.

Janine waited until Stephanie was out of earshot. "So, what's going on between you and Noah?" she asked.

Rachel gaped at her. "I don't know what you mean. Noah and I once lived close to each other. We were friends."

"Oh, hon. I see the way he looks at you. That's more than friendship."

Rachel's cheeks flamed. "I think you are mistaken."

Janine covered her hands. "Perhaps, and I certainly don't mean to pry. It's just that I haven't seen Noah show this much attention to a woman before. The poor man suffered so much with his wife passing away at such a young age. I've always thought something in his past was keeping him from finding the love he needed in his life. When I heard about Olivia, I figured she'd been the one for him. But now that I've met you, seen the way he looks at you, well, I'm positive he has feelings for you."

Rachel ducked her head. "Noah is my *gut* friend, but that is all. Our worlds are very different, and I do not plan to marry again."

Sympathy replaced the curiosity on Janine's face. "Oh, honey, I won't pretend to know what you've been through or about the differences between you and Noah, but I will tell you this. Life is too short to let anything stand in the way of finding the one you are supposed to be with."

Noah sat up slowly. The room spun and he closed his eyes until his nausea subsided.

What happened earlier slowly crawled through the fog surrounding his brain, and he clambered to his feet. Rachel. He needed to make sure she was okay.

His feet stumbled slightly, and he clutched the sofa to catch himself. When he got his legs underneath him, Noah hobbled down the hall to where Rachel sat beside Janine.

The moment Rachel spotted him, she jumped from her seat and rushed to his side, the concern in her eyes warming his heart.

"I'm okay," he said. Still, she stared at him, her forehead creased into a worried frown. He couldn't imagine how bad he looked.

"Come here and sit down," Janine ordered, and he sank to the chair she supplied him. "You need to be in a hospital bed." Though the words came out gruff, Noah understood they were from the heart.

"I feel much better now that I rested." He glanced out the windows in front of the station where the streetlights kept the twilight at bay. Another day drew to a close. Another day without finding Eva. "Anything new?"

Janine clearly didn't believe him. "Cole's trying to get some shut-eye in the break room. Ryan's over at the Yoder place, and Aden's working in the conference room with Walker. And you look as if you need something to eat. Rachel and I had pizza earlier. I'll go warm you a couple of slices. It'll help your energy level."

Noah knew better than to argue. "Thanks," he murmured as she headed away.

Walker and Aden stepped out into the hall.

"Glad to see you amongst the living again," Walker told him.

"Thanks, I think." Noah grinned. "Anything show up on the prints?"

The excitement on Aden's face promised good news. "Oh yeah. We've ID'd both men from IAFIS. They're a couple of thugs operating out of Billings."

"Billings?" Noah didn't hide his surprise. "That's more than five hundred miles away. What are they doing this far north, and more important, what do they want with Rachel and Eva?"

"Good question." Walker crooked a thumb to the conference room. "Aden and I have these guys' records. We've been running through them to see if we can find some connection. So far, we've come up empty-handed."

"Let me take a look. Maybe a fresh set of eyes will help," Noah said.

Walker didn't seem nearly as convinced. "Are you sure you're feeling up to it? Janine is right. You should be at the hospital."

"I'm fine," he insisted and shifted to Rachel. "It's been hours since you slept. You should try."

She shook her head. "I am too keyed up. Besides, I want to help. These men are coming after Eva and me. I can't sit around and do nothing."

Her courage wasn't a surprise. "All right. Let's see if we can figure out who these men are working for."

"Not so fast, mister. You need to eat something first." Janine handed him a plate containing a couple of slices of pizza.

"I can eat while we work." When she arched a brow, he made the cross my heart symbol. "I promise."

"I'm holding you to it," Janine tossed over her shoulder as she rounded her desk.

With a chuckle, Noah winced as he put weight on his swollen leg.

In the conference room, a couple of laptops had been set up.

"Where's Megan?" Noah asked.

"Out on a call," Walker said. "We may have a break on our John Doe's case. Some hikers near the Salish Mountains on the northern side of Lake Koocanusa called to say they found a wallet on one of the more remote trails. Megan is on her way there now."

"That's some ways from where John Doe drove off the bridge and from where we located his body. How do you think the wallet ended up there?" Noah asked.

"No idea. It could have been dragged there by an animal," Aden suggested. "Although there was no evidence of an animal attack on John Doe's body."

Noah couldn't get the feeling out of his head that John Doe's case was somehow related to what was happening with Rachel and Eva.

Aden typed something into one of the laptops and pulled up a photo. "Meet Drew Parker." Noah stared at the man. "He has a rap sheet as long as my arm. Mostly petty stuff. A few assaults. Nothing like this, though."

"What about the second man?" Noah asked.

"His partner is Marvin Arnold. His rap sheet almost

matches Parker's to a tee, and get this—" Aden paused for a second "—our George Mason grew up in Billings, too. Kind of a coincidence, don't you think?"

"So why are two, possibly three, thugs from Billings here in Eagle's Nest?" Noah said to himself.

"That's the question we need to answer, and soon," Walker said. "So far, Mason isn't talking. What about known associates? Who do these guys hang out with?"

Aden pulled up Parker's file on the laptop. He sat back and stared at the screen. "Whoa. This guy's involved with a heavy hitter."

Noah glanced over Aden's shoulder. "Holden Mc-Graff?" Noah couldn't believe the man had ties to a suspected crime syndicate boss.

"Who is Holden McGraff?" Rachel asked.

"One of the biggest crime bosses in Montana. He's involved in gambling and extortion. Human trafficking. This guy is a serious criminal, and no one's ever tied him to a single one of his crimes."

Aden pulled up a photo of Holden. He lived on a thousand-acre ranch outside of Billings. From outward appearances, he was a polished member of the elite, but his name was tied to a lot of illegal activity. If this guy was involved, they had reason to be worried.

"Do you recognize this guy?" Noah asked Rachel. He could see from the disappointment on her face she didn't.

"It's okay," he said gently. "Believe it or not, we are making progress. We just have to figure out how Holden McGraff fits into all of this."

Walker's cell phone rang. He answered and listened for a moment. "How did it end up so far away from the accident?" The conversation captured Noah's attention. "All right. Let's see if we can get in touch with this guy's next of kin. Find out why he was out there alone." Walker disconnected the call.

"The wallet's our John Doe's," Noah said, anticipating Walker's answer.

"It is. A man by the name of Allan Miller. Megan's trying to find the man's next of kin, but guess where he lives?"

Noah didn't have to guess. "Billings," he supplied, and Walker gave him a *bingo* look.

"Yep. I'm not one to believe in coincidences. Especially not ones this big."

"Noah," Rachel whispered in a strangled tone.

He twisted to her. "What's wrong?"

"Allan Miller. A. Miller." It took a second for the truth to dawn. Was it possible Allan Miller was the same man who was supposed to meet with Eva?

NINETEEN

Rachel felt the blood drain from her face.

"This could be the guy who met with Eva." Noah shifted to Aden. "Can you get a DMV photo pulled up of Allan Miller?"

"I can." Aden typed some words into the laptop and a driver's license photo popped up.

Rachel stared at the photo. Something about the man seemed vaguely familiar, or perhaps was she merely grasping for straws.

"Do you recognize him?" Noah asked, searching her face.

She shook her head. "I can't be sure. There is something familiar about him, but I don't know why." She squinted at the photo, but no answers came.

"Find out what you can about this man. We need answers now," Walker told Aden and headed for the door.

"Where are you going?" Aden asked as he continued typing.

"To speak with the coroner. Have him take a closer look at Allan Miller's autopsy report. I don't think this guy died accidentally. Not after what's happened here today."

Rachel sank to one of the chairs. They'd believed Allan Miller was the young man Eva had been seeing in secret, but this man was middle-aged. So why was Eva meeting with him?

"What do you think his connection is to Eva?" she asked, unable to connect her sister to the man in the photo.

Noah sat next to her. "At this point, we can't be sure. From the time of death the coroner gave us, it's safe to say Miller entered the lake before Eva was taken. Which seems to indicate he didn't have anything to do with her disappearance."

"So why did he wish to meet with her?"

The bleakness in Noah's eyes scared her. "I've no idea. Maybe we should speak to Anna again. Perhaps she's remembered something she didn't before."

"This is odd," Aden murmured half to himself. "Allan Miller is the owner of one of the largest oil companies in Montana. Big Sky Oil has rigs all around the state, but get this—they've been drilling around the Eagle's Nest area for a few months now."

Rachel stared at a grainy photo from a news article written before Big Sky Oil began drilling. Miller stood in front of some drilling equipment smiling into the camera. Why did he look so familiar? There would be no reason why she would have come into contact with an oil tycoon. Still, if what they believed were true, Miller had reached out to Eva at some point. Wanted to see her. Why?

Rachel studied the photo more closely. She didn't recognize the countryside in the background. It could be anywhere around the county, including close to the Amish community.

"If Miller came to Eagle's Nest to run the operation, why hasn't someone reported him missing by now?" Noah asked. "It's been days at the very least."

Aden shook his head. "Good question." He glanced at his watch. "I know those rigs run twenty-four/seven most of the time. I'll call Walker and update him on what we have. Maybe there's someone at the rig site who can provide us with answers."

"Good idea," Noah said. He turned to Rachel and scanned her face. "We need to find someplace where you can get a good night's sleep. We can't go back to the Yoders', since we'd be putting them in jeopardy. Hang tight for a second. I'll be right back."

He left the room. Rachel continued to stare at the man in the photo. How did he connect to Eva? Why hadn't her sister mentioned anything about their meeting? And more important, why had Eva chosen to see an *Englisch* man when she was sure she was ready to embrace the Amish way of life?

The garage door slid closed. Noah sat up.

"I don't believe anyone followed me," Janine told him as she glanced into the back seat where he and Rachel had crouched out of sight.

"Thanks, Janine. To be safe, I'll take a look around inside first."

Janine handed him her house key.

When Janine had first suggested he and Rachel stay with her, Noah had been reluctant to put her in harm's way. As a former deputy herself, Janine had been quick to inform him she could take care of herself and they needed someplace out of sight to stash Rachel. They'd devised a plan that kept him and Rachel hidden from view until they reached Janine's house.

Unlocking the door, Noah slipped into Janine's kitchen. A noise came from the living room, followed by footsteps. Janine's Siberian husky, Elsa, ran into the kitchen to investigate.

"Hey Elsa, you remember me?" After a second's hesitation, the dog sniffed his hand. Noah patted her head. "Good girl. Have you seen any bad guys?"

The dog wagged her tail in answer and followed Noah through the house as he checked each room.

Janine's home was on a quiet street in Eagle's Nest. She lived alone, except for the dog.

With another pat for the dog, Noah headed out to the garage. "All's quiet. I think Elsa is doing her job."

Janine and Rachel got out and headed inside. In the living room, Janine clicked on the gas-powered fireplace.

"Make yourself at home. I'll whip us up something for dinner, or do you want to rest for a bit?" she asked Rachel, who shook her head.

"That is very kind of you, but I'm fine. I'll help you with the meal."

Janine waved her off. "Nonsense. You stay here and warm up. I think I have some meat loaf in the freezer. I'll thaw it out. Won't take a minute."

When it was just the two of them, Noah sat next to Rachel. "You're safe here. No one followed us, and even if they did, they would have no way of knowing we were with Janine."

She smiled into his eyes, and he lost his heart again.

"*Denki*, Noah. I know you are doing all you can to protect me and bring Eva home."

The weariness of the job sank deep into his soul. He'd tried to convince himself he was doing God's will, but more and more lately, the things he saw daily corroded his being. The simple Amish ways called to him. Had ever since he left the community behind. No matter what the future might bring, he would find Eva. He'd do that because he cared for Rachel and her sister.

"What is it?" she asked, seeing the things he couldn't hide.

He shook his head. "I don't know. Maybe I'm just tired," he said, but the weariness felt much more profound than something physical.

She touched his hand. "There's more."

Looking deep into her eyes, he wished for so much more. "I guess I was remembering when I lived near you. Things were so much simpler. I knew what I wanted from life. How did it all go so wrong?" She drew in a breath but didn't look away.

He'd known he loved Rachel. Knew what he wanted for his future. Then it all ended.

For so long, he'd been angry with his dad. Even though he'd been wrong to push his wishes on his son, Noah had made his share of mistakes and done his part in fracturing the relationship.

"You were very young, Noah, and things appear different when you look back at them. You brush the problems aside and see only the happy moments."

"I was the happiest I've ever been..." He touched her cheek, and she swallowed visibly. The look in her eyes became distant, and she rose.

"But you were not Amish. It would not have worked out for us. Perhaps for a while, until you grew tired of our way of life and left." She stopped for a breath. "We were not meant to be together," she said gently. "Daniel was my husband, and I loved him, and you, well, you are doing good work with the sheriff's department. You must find a way to be at peace with that."

She spun away and left him alone with his misery. Each of her words struck like a stone to his heart. Life had a cruel way of working out sometimes, but perhaps she was right. It was for the best. He was damaged emotionally, living with guilt.

Drawing in a steadying breath, Noah closed his eyes. So what was he supposed to do with all these feelings he still had for her? He knew she would be better off without him, but he needed God's help to get over these feelings.

"Father, there is so much turmoil in me. I don't know what to do anymore. Open my eyes and show me the path You would have me follow. Help me let her go when this case ends, because I don't think I have it in my heart to lose her again."

TWENTY

Rachel slept fitfully. Too many troubling thoughts gathered in her head. She could see the pain on Noah's face each time she closed her eyes. She still cared for him. It broke her heart to think she could not be the woman he needed her to be. There would be no family for them. No happy ending.

The smell of coffee wafted in from the kitchen. Rachel swung her legs off the bed, the carpet warm on her feet, so unlike the cold floors of her house. When she thought about the place where she'd grown up, she longed to return to a time before this nightmare began.

A new day was in the works outside. Another one passed without any news about Eva. The thought of her sister never coming home was just too much to consider. Grabbing the dress she'd borrowed from Sadie from the chair, Rachel dressed quickly. Brushing out her hair, she repinned it. As she stared out the window that looked into Janine's backyard, a flash of color caught her attention and she moved closer. A shadow appeared near the spruce tree by the fence. Rachel ducked out of sight. It couldn't be them. How would they possibly know where to find her?

With her heart pounding she ran from the room and straight into Noah's chest.

"What's wrong?" he asked, concerned. Noah clasped

her arm, his gaze flicking over her face. "Rachel, tell me what happened."

Getting the words to come out became an almost impossible task. She pointed to the room. "I thought I saw someone near the tree out back," she managed. Letting her go, Noah hurried past her into the room she'd just left, and she followed. He eased to the window and peered out.

Rachel glanced over his shoulder. There was nothing there. "I saw movement and noticed a shadow by the tree. It's gone now."

Noah called for assistance. "Thanks. I don't think I'm a hundred percent ready to take on these guys again alone." Ending the call, Noah took her arm and urged her to the living room. "We need to get away from the window."

She noticed how pale he was for the first time. "Are you *oke*?" Rachel forgot the shadow. Noah appeared so pale. With his arm still in a sling, he favored his injured leg. He'd come close to dying the day before.

He smiled briefly. "I'm fine. It's probably not them anyway. Janine was pretty positive we weren't followed last night." Still, doubts showed on his face. "Unless they've been watching the station long enough to become acquainted with everyone who works there. Maybe they figured out we'd try to stash you someplace they'd never think to look." He blew out a sigh and ran a hand over his eyes. "In any case, I'm just not strong enough to take them on alone. But we should be okay here. The house is like Fort Knox. As a former deputy herself, Janine made sure she installed all the latest security devices when she moved in here a few years ago."

Rachel looked around. "Where is she?"

"At work. She drove to the station about an hour ago. That was her I just spoke with."

Outside, tires screeched to a halt in front of the house,

and Noah parted the window curtains. "That's Ryan and Cole."

The deputies knocked once, and Noah let them in.

Noah explained what Rachel had seen. "Near the fence at the back of the house."

"We'll check it out," Cole told them.

Noah closed the door and faced her. His gaze held hers.

She turned away, moved to the kitchen and poured more coffee while Noah stayed near the window.

A knock rattled the door, and she jumped. Noah pulled the door open. Cole came inside and Rachel carried her coffee to the living room to listen. "Were there footprints?" Noah asked.

"Yes. One set. Someone was there."

"Do you think it was one of them?" Noah asked as he held her gaze.

"With everything that's happened, it would be foolish to dismiss the possibility, but whoever was there is gone now."

"What happens next?" she asked, her voice but a whisper.

Cole answered, "Ryan and I will speak with the neighbors to see if they saw anything unusual this morning. When we're done, you and Noah can ride to the station with us."

"And until then, you should try and eat something. Janine made breakfast earlier and set a plate aside for you," Noah said.

"I'll check in with Ryan," Cole said before heading outside.

The thought of food had little appeal with Eva foremost in her thoughts. She hadn't seen her sister since Sunday. Eva must be terrified. They lived a simple life, or so Rachel had thought, but the secrets they'd uncovered about Eva made her wonder what other things her sister had hidden from her. There was a reason why these men wanted her and Eva, and she believed it had something to do with the young man Eva was seeing. In her heart she knew something far more terrifying was waiting out there, ready to swallow her up.

"That is good news," Noah said once Ryan finished explaining what they'd found out at the drill site.

"I think we're finally getting somewhere. We're on our way in now. We'll see you soon." Ryan ended the call.

Noah put the phone in his pocket and faced Rachel. She sat at the conference room table, glued to his every word. "That was Ryan. Allan Miller's stepson, Peter Hargrave, has agreed to come in and speak with us."

When Cole and Ryan arrived at the local drill site for Big Sky Oil, the graveyard shift workers hadn't been much help. No one remembered seeing Miller recently, but they all knew Miller's stepson, Peter Hargrave, ran the operation. Megan had contacted Hargrave and asked him to come in. She hadn't mentioned anything about Miller being deceased. They'd want to gauge his reaction when they informed him of the news.

"I wonder why no one reported this man missing." Rachel vocalized the question troubling him, as well.

He shook his head. "Hopefully, we'll have some answers when the stepson gets here. In the meantime, I want to speak with Anna again and see if maybe she remembers something more about the young man." Noah glanced at his watch. "Hargrave will be here at three. Aden just arrived to start his shift. I'll grab him."

He hesitated. Each time Rachel was out in public the chances of these men taking her doubled. Still, he didn't want to let her out of his sight.

"I'll be fine," she said.

He wasn't nearly as sure. Noah noticed Walker coming into the station. The sheriff had gone to check on Theresa and get some sleep. Noah hadn't spoken to him since he left to talk with the coroner. "Let me have a word with Walker first." Noah headed for the door, but the sheriff entered the room before Noah could leave.

Walker's grim expression was not encouraging. With a quick look back at Rachel, he stepped out into the hall with the sheriff.

"The coroner took another look at the autopsy results in light of what we've discovered about our victim. There was a head injury that he initially believed was caused by Miller's head hitting the steering wheel. After further examination, the angle of the injury doesn't align with that hypothesis. He believes someone may have hit Miller before he entered the car. Chances are he was unconscious when the vehicle went into the lake."

"In other words, we're looking at a homicide," Noah concluded.

"I believe so. Somehow or other, these two cases are connected. We have to figure out how." Walker glanced into the conference room. "How's she holding up?"

"Barely keeping it together. We sure need something to break our way."

Walker nodded. "Hopefully, the stepson will give us something." Walker looked him up and down. "How are you doing?"

In truth, he felt like a truck had hit him. Just walking proved a struggle, but he had to stay strong for Rachel. He couldn't afford to get removed from the case due to health issues.

"I'm okay. I'm going to grab Aden and take a ride to

the Lapps' place again to see if Anna thought of something she didn't before."

Walker nodded. "Go. Let's hope the girl remembers something."

"I'm taking Rachel with me. I know it's not ideal, but I don't want to let her out of my sight."

"Keep an eye on her. These guys have proven they can get to her at any time."

Though he realized the danger, hearing Walker say that intensified Noah's worry.

"I will." With a sick feeling settling in the pit of his stomach, Noah gathered Rachel and went to find Aden.

Stepping outside with Aden at his side, Noah's gaze shot around the area. The traffic in the street in front of the station appeared light. Nothing out of the ordinary.

He swiveled to the door and motioned for Rachel, quickly ushering her into the patrol vehicle. He shut the door and slid into the passenger side while Aden took the wheel.

As they pulled out onto the street, Noah kept his focus on the passing vehicles. So far, so good.

Once they left the city limits, a glance in the side mirror proved they were not being followed.

Noah turned in his seat and forced a smile for Rachel. "Relax. There's no one there."

She leaned back, letting out a relieved breath.

The drive to the Lapps' home was a silent one, so Noah thought about what they knew so far. One question in particular stuck in his head. Why hadn't anyone reported Miller missing?

Aden pulled onto the long drive. After the car stopped, Noah hopped out and opened Rachel's door.

With her at his side, the fear that seemed to be embedded on her face brought his protective instincts to the surface.

With his hand resting gently on her back, they headed up the steps to the porch where Aden waited.

Noah nodded and his partner knocked on the door.

Footfalls headed to the door, and Kathryn opened it, her brows slanted downward in a frown.

"Mrs. Lapp, we're sorry to interrupt your day, but can we speak to Anna again?" Noah asked.

The woman eyed them for the longest time. She silently opened the door wider and stepped away.

They stepped inside, and Noah closed the door.

"I'll get Anna." Kathryn pointed to the living room. "Please have a seat."

"Denki," Rachel murmured, and the older woman's face softened.

"Is there any news on Eva?" Rachel shook her head. "I am praying for her," the older woman whispered and hurried away.

Rachel sank to one of the rockers in front of the wood-stove along with Noah while Aden kept his post near the window.

Minutes passed before Kathryn returned with her daughter.

Anna's fearful gaze shot between the three of them as Rachel rose to her feet. Noah did the same.

"Did you find Eva?" she asked, her eyes darting between them.

Noah pivoted to Rachel. He understood the young woman might feel more comfortable speaking with her.

"Nay, we have not found Eva yet," she said. "We are wondering if perhaps you may have remembered something more that might be useful in bringing Eva home."

Anna's eyes grew wide. "I have told you what I remember."

Noah's first instinct was to push, but he didn't want the young woman to shut down.

"Perhaps there is something you do not think is important," Rachel said and glanced his way. Noah could see the despair in her eyes, but she pushed on. "We have nothing, Anna, and it has been days. Time is running out for Eva. Please, think about what Eva mentioned about this man. Is there anything you might have forgotten?"

The young woman shook her head, ready to say no, then stopped.

"*Jah*, there is something," she murmured, almost to herself. Anna drew in a breath. "Eva mentioned the young man said he was about to come into some money soon. But he needed her help for it to happen. Eva laughed about it, thinking it would be an adventure."

Noah's gaze shot to Rachel. He could see it in her eyes. She'd come to the same conclusion as he. Did the young man mean he needed to kidnap Eva and Rachel to come into the money? If so, why was someone willing to pay him to snatch the sisters? What exactly was the end game?

TWENTY-ONE

"Is this important?" Anna asked, her brow furrowed as she glanced around at them.

"I think so," Rachel told her. They just had to figure out how. "Eva never mentioned anything about what this young man looked like?" It hurt that her sister had kept something this big secret from her.

Anna shook her head. "I'm sorry, but no." The worst possible news. Someone had taken Eva for money, and they had no idea how to connect the pieces together.

"Thank you for your help, Anna." Noah nodded toward the two women. They started for the door, a sinking feeling growing inside Rachel.

"Wait!" Anna called after them. "I don't think she was serious about this young man. Eva was flattered by the attention he gave her, but not serious. She was excited about becoming the *kinner*'s teacher and joining the church in a few weeks' time. And she was still on her *rumspringa*." Anna lifted her shoulders. "She was having a little fun before she settled down."

Rachel wanted to believe this with all her heart.

"After all, she only knew him for a few days. How could she be serious?" Anna told them.

"*Denki*, Anna, Kathryn," Rachel said, and both women nodded.

"You'll let me know when you find her?" Anna stopped before adding, "No matter what, please let me know."

Outside, the afternoon grew ugly. Dark gray clouds gathered and released flat snowflakes in a downpour.

Noah glanced up at the dreary sky. "It isn't much, but I think we can agree that, whoever this young man is, he's behind all of this." He held the door open for her and Rachel slid into the back seat. The door shut. Both men climbed into the front.

A thought occurred to Rachel. "Have you spoken to my *mamm*?" she asked, curious if Beth knew what was happening to her daughters.

Noah looked at her. "No. We have men sitting on her at your aunt's house, but we didn't want to alarm them unnecessarily, and we figured if Beth knew what was happening, she would want to come and help. Even though there's been no threat to her life, it's safer for her where she is. Why do you ask?"

"I wondered if perhaps Eva might have mentioned something to her about this young man. Eva wrote *Mamm* a couple of times. I think I should tell her what is happening. She needs to know."

The doubt on Noah's face assured her he didn't believe Eva told their *mamm*. In the past, she would agree, but if there was a chance she'd mentioned something to Beth, they needed to know.

Noah faced forward. "We can't afford to dismiss anything, however small. I'll get in touch with the sheriff's department in Alamosa and have Beth call the station so you can speak with her."

She closed her eyes, dreading the call. *Where are you, Eva?* Her sister's sweet face appeared before her. She'd give anything to see that smile again.

"Do you see that?" Her eyes shot open at the tension in Aden's voice.

"Yeah, I do," Noah answered, his voice strained.

Both men were looking in their respective mirrors. Rachel whirled around. A car followed some distance behind them. Her heart flew to her throat.

"Get down," Noah urged her, and she crouched as low as she could.

"What is happening?" she murmured, her imagination going wild.

"We don't know yet. It could be an innocent driver, but at this point, we can't afford to take any chances," Noah told her.

"The vehicle is speeding up," Aden warned. He unholstered his sidearm. Noah did the same. "They're going to pass."

"Stay low, Rachel." The edge in Noah's voice was frightening.

She could hear the vehicle as it drew closer.

"They're switching lanes now. I see two men inside," Aden said, his voice tight.

Rachel peered out the window and watched a small dark blue car ease alongside them. From where she lay, she couldn't see the men at all.

It felt like forever before the car passed them. Noah let out a breath. "I'm calling it in." He grabbed his phone and put it on speaker. Janine answered, and he gave her the license plate number.

Rachel eased to a sitting position. The car was now some distance in front of them.

"Hang on a second, Noah," Janine told him. "I'm running the plate now... The vehicle was reported stolen two days ago near Eureka."

"This could be our guys," Aden said. "But we can't

afford a showdown with Rachel here and Noah still not a hundred percent."

Noah gave Janine their location. "We need immediate backup."

"Megan's heading your way now. Hang back until she can intercept the vehicle."

"Will do," Noah said as the patrol vehicle edged around the curve in the road. They'd barely cleared it when Aden braked hard. The car had stopped sideways in the road. "Back up," Noah shouted. Aden shoved the patrol vehicle into Reverse. With his eyes glued on the road behind them he whipped the car around.

Rachel lurched forward in her seat, the safety restraint locking hard. She braced herself against the door as the patrol vehicle flew into Drive and headed back the way they'd come.

"What's happening?" Janine's frantic voice echoed inside the vehicle.

Noah had just begun to explain when another vehicle appeared out of nowhere and headed straight for them. The driver whipped the car sideways in the road, exactly like the other car. Aden stopped fast. They were pinned in. "We're trapped. We need help now, Janine."

"Walker's on his way there. Hang on, guys."

Two men in the car in front of them got out through the passenger side. They were putting the vehicle between them for protection.

"They're armed," Aden said as a barrel flashed over the top of the car.

"Stay low," Noah urged Rachel and glanced behind them. The other car eased closer. The two men inside followed the example of their cohorts and slipped from the vehicle and into position.

"They're going to attack. Our backup won't make it in time," Aden said as he eyed the car in front of them.

"Noah…" Rachel's voice was filled with emotion and he tried to reassure her.

"It's going to be okay. We just have to hold them off for a little while longer." Noah turned to Aden and pointed behind them. "I'll take these guys if you can handle the ones in front of us."

"I've got them. What say we try to shake them out of their comfort zone?"

"On three." Noah eased onto the back seat and counted off. Before he got to three, the men behind them opened fire. The back window shattered. Noah covered Rachel to keep her protected from flying glass. Shards embedded in his hair. Nicked his face. One of the shooters took out the back tires.

Noah waited until the shooting stopped before emptying his mag and sending the men ducking for cover.

"I'm going to take out their tires," Aden said and fired. Both driver-side tires blew. The two men wouldn't be getting away.

With the full mag snapped in place, Noah aimed for the front tire, but the men opened fire, forcing him to duck low.

In the distance, two sets of sirens could be heard. Megan and Walker were close.

The two men he'd been shooting at jumped into the car. The driver floored the engine, roared passed them on the side of the road and flew to the car in front. The two stranded men leaped inside.

"They're trying to get away," Noah said and punched the radio on his shoulder. He quickly updated Walker and Megan. They couldn't let the men escape. If they did, their only lead in finding Eva would disappear. That couldn't happen.

One of the men hung out the window and shot at the cruiser, striking its radiator and rendering them dead in the water. The car sped down the road and out of sight.

Behind them, flashing lights gained on them. Megan flew past them in pursuit while Walker pulled up and got out.

"Everyone okay?" Walker asked.

Noah got out and opened Rachel's door. She stumbled and he clasped her arm. "You're okay," he whispered against her ear. "I promise you're okay."

Rachel pulled in a shaky breath and pushed at his chest. When Noah let her go, she turned away. The action seemed to confirm the truth. No matter how much he loved her, the time had passed for them.

"Let's get you back to the station," he said, unable to disguise his hurt. Rachel slid into the back seat of Walker's car and Noah got in beside her, while Aden took the front seat.

As Walker eased the vehicle toward the station, Noah didn't want to worry Rachel further, but he hoped Miller's stepson could provide them with answers because right now, they had very little to go on and time was running out.

His phone rang again. Megan. "There's no sign of the car. I'll check the side roads and see if can find them."

"Copy that," Noah responded, knowing that the likelihood was slim.

Throughout the drive to the station, Noah was on edge. The attacks were increasing. These men were more determined than ever. What were they after? They'd torn apart Rachel's home looking for something. He had a feeling whatever they'd been searching for wasn't there.

Janine met them at the door of the station. "Sheriff Solomon from Alamosa is on the line. He has Rachel's mother with him."

Rachel reached for his hand. He couldn't imagine how difficult it would be for Rachel to tell her mother about Eva.

"Let's take it in the conference room," Noah said, and together they went to the room. He picked up the phone. "Sheriff Solomon, I have Rachel Albrecht here for Beth." He handed the phone to Rachel and started to leave.

"No. Please stay," she said, her eyes pleading.

Noah sat beside her and listened as she explained to Beth about Eva's disappearance.

"I'm sorry, *Mamm*. I know you trusted Eva's care to me and I let you down."

While he couldn't hear Beth's response, he knew the woman well enough to be sure she wouldn't let her daughter take the blame for what happened.

"Do you remember anything unusual in Eva's letters? Did she mention seeing a young man?" Rachel listened. Her shoulders slumped. Beth had no idea about the young man.

Tears spilled from Rachel's eyes. "No, *Mamm*, you should stay where you are for now. As soon as Eva is safely home, I will let the sheriff know." She brushed the back of her hand across her eyes. "I love you, too. And I will see you soon."

She hung up the phone and covered her face with her hands and wept.

Noah hesitated only a second, then gathered her close, holding her while she cried.

"I'm *oke*," she whispered at last. "It was just hard."

Noah brushed his thumbs across her cheeks. "Did Beth mention anything unusual about Eva's letters?"

Rachel shook her head. "No, she said Eva mostly mentioned things that happened in the classroom."

The sinking feeling inside Noah's gut assured him they were missing something vital. But what?

Someone opened the door and Noah turned. Janine entered the room with Walker and another man. Peter Hargrave. Noah wasn't sure what he'd been expecting, but Hargrave was a clean-cut young man who didn't quite fit the part of someone who managed roughnecks.

"Do you mind staying with Janine while we interview this man?" he asked Rachel softly.

"Not at all." She rose and followed Janine out of the room. Noah watched her go, acutely aware of the number of hours that had passed since Eva went missing.

Please, God, help us find Eva soon.

"Noah, this is Peter Hargrave." Walker introduced him to the man.

"Nice to meet you, Deputy Warren." Hargrave extended his hand. Noah rose and shook it.

"Why don't you have a seat, Mr. Hargrave? Can I get you anything? Coffee?" Walker asked, but the young man shook his head. Pulling out a chair, he sat.

"What's this about, Sheriff?" he asked, curiosity in his eyes.

Noah moved to the end of the table where he could watch Hargrave's reactions.

Walker lowered his frame to the edge of the table. "I have some bad news," he said and paused for a moment.

Hargrave glanced from Walker to Noah. "What is it?"

"It's your stepfather. I'm sorry to have to tell you this, but he's dead." Walker delivered the news with as much tact as possible, then he sat back and watched Hargrave's expression, as did Noah.

The man's eyes widened in disbelief. "I beg your pardon?" his voice was barely audible. So far, all the correct reactions.

"Your stepfather's car slid off the Lake Koocanusa Bridge. I'm afraid he's dead."

Hargrave appeared to struggle to take it in. "But that's not possible. I spoke with him last week. He was heading up to the high country to hunt elk like he does every year around this time."

"What day was that, exactly?" Noah asked.

Hargrave thought about it for a second. "Last Monday. He had the car packed for the trip. He wasn't planning to go home to Billings, but driving straight to his hunting cabin instead."

"And that's the last time anyone heard from him?" Walker asked.

Hargrave glanced from Noah to the sheriff. "As far as I know. Is there something else you haven't mentioned?" he asked, guessing the truth.

Walker hesitated briefly. "I'm afraid there is. I'm sorry to have to tell you this, Mr. Hargrave, but it appears someone murdered your stepfather."

The younger man stared at him as if he hadn't heard him correctly. "Murdered? But that's impossible. My stepfather doesn't have an enemy around. Everyone loves him." Tears formed in the man's eyes. He certainly appeared genuinely upset.

"We're still investigating. At this point, we'll have a dive team go into the lake to see if we can retrieve the car." Walker stopped for a second before asking the necessary question. "You'll understand that I need you to account for your time starting with that Monday."

The younger man wiped his eyes and slowly nodded. "Of course. I was where I always am. At the rig. Allan gave the rig to me to run, and it's my baby. You can ask the men who work for me. I'm rarely ever gone. I have a camper on site. It's where I stay."

Walker gave a curt nod. "I appreciate your cooperation. Can you think of anyone who might wish to harm your stepfather?"

Hargrave didn't hesitate. "No, everyone loves him. I can't imagine who would do this."

Walker's gaze connected with Noah's and Noah could almost read what he was thinking. Someone had wanted Miller dead enough to accomplish it.

"As soon as we have any news, I'll let you know," Walker told Hargrave.

"Thank you." Hargrave stared at the table. "Can you tell me when I can see my dad? I want to make sure he has a proper funeral. I'm the only family he has."

Walker took out a piece of paper and wrote down a number. "Call this number. The coroner will let you know when he can release the body." Walker held out his hand, and Hargrave shook it. "Again, I am sorry for your loss."

"Thank you." Hargrave nodded to Noah. "If I can help you with the investigation in any way, please let me know. I want to find the monster who did this to my dad."

Hargrave stood and headed for the door when Noah thought of something else.

"Just a second," he said and Hargrave turned back. "Are your mother and Miller still married?" From the way Hargrave talked, it was just him and Miller.

The young man rubbed a hand across his eyes. "No, they're not. They divorced when I was fourteen. I chose to stay with Allan."

"Does your mother live in Billings?" Noah asked.

Hargrave shook his head. "No, she moved to Wyoming to be close to friends. That's where she grew up." Hargrave shrugged and headed out the door.

"I'll walk you out," Noah said and fell into step beside him. As they drew near the dispatch station, Noah noticed

Rachel sitting beside Janine. He stopped and asked her how she was feeling because he wanted to see her reaction to Hargrave.

"I'm fine." She glanced at Hargrave briefly, but didn't appear to recognize him. Noah needed to be sure. She'd been distraught before and might not have gotten a good look at him.

Noah shifted his attention to the younger man, who had a polite smile on his face, but he didn't show any undue reaction to Rachel.

On an impulse, Noah led Hargrave past the holding cell where George Mason was confined. Mason wore the same glare on his face that he used for everyone who walked by. Hargrave never spared him a single glance.

Holding back his frustration, Noah led the way to the front door and held it open. "Thank you again for coming in, Mr. Hargrave. As soon as we know anything at all, we'll be in touch."

"I appreciate it. Please find out who did this, Deputy Warren. Allan was a good man, and I owe him my life. He was the one person who was there for me growing up. He deserves better." Hargrave swiped his hand across his eyes and headed out into the wintry day.

Noah waited until the man climbed into his pickup truck before stopping by the dispatch station to let Rachel know he would return in a minute. Then he headed to the conference room.

"He seemed genuinely upset by the news of his stepfather's death," Noah said, pacing the room.

Walker agreed. "He did. I'll have Aden check out his story, but I think we have to keep looking. Let's check into people who were fired by Miller, whether at the rig here or one of his other locations. Maybe someone had a grudge against Miller that got out of control."

It was possible, but Noah couldn't understand how a grudge against Miller was tied into what was happening to Eva and Rachel. The connection was there. They just had to figure it out before it was too late.

TWENTY-TWO

So far, each new clue they'd uncovered had ended in a dead end and left them no closer to finding Eva than the first day she disappeared.

"I know you're supposed to go into work at the bulk foods store tomorrow, but in light of what happened today, I don't think it's a good idea."

Neither did she, but she didn't want Esther to have to make the trip in such weather conditions.

"I realize this is not the best time, but Esther depends on me. She has no one else."

The battle raging inside him became clear. Rachel would be exposed at the store. Vulnerable.

"I won't let her down, Noah." She stood her ground.

He stared into her eyes for the longest time before sighing. "All right, but I'll want Cole and Ryan there with us at all times. And if the weather continues like this, we won't stay long."

She smiled up at him. "*Denki*, Noah." He'd risked so much already to protect her. *Gott, please shield us.*

Noah touched her cheek and she closed her eyes. Every time she was near him, what she wanted and what was possible warred with each other.

"Rachel…" She shivered at the husky sound of her name coming from his lips. She opened her eyes. Noah stepped closer. The longing in his eyes matched that in her heart. With a breathless sigh, he kissed her gently. A sigh escaped as she kissed him back because she still cared for him. His touch was familiar. Warm. Filled with promises that could never be.

With a sob, she ended the kiss and stepped back. His hand fell to his side. The hurt on his face was hard to take.

She covered her lips with her hand. She could still feel his touch there.

"I'm sorry," he murmured. Her heart broke at his apology.

Drawing in a much-needed breath, Rachel struggled for solid ground.

The strained silence between them hurt. She tried to think of something to say fill the void when all she could think about was how much she wanted him to kiss her again.

"Did Mr. Miller's stepson offer any hint of who did this to him?" she asked, her voice strained.

Noah cleared his throat without looking at her. "Not really. We're checking to see if someone Miller fired might hold a grudge against him. Walker called the local PD in Billings. They're going to Miller's home today." He looked at his watch. "I'll see if I can arrange to have food delivered," he said and left the room.

Rachel struggled to keep back tears. It hurt terribly to think there would never be a future for them. Those two young people who fell in love all those years ago would once again be separated by circumstances they couldn't control. Only this time it was final.

From Cole's position at the rear of the store, he could see anyone coming and going in that direction. Ryan, stationed past the phone shanty, had a clear view of the front of the bulk foods store. Still, that little niggling of unease in Noah's head wouldn't let him relax.

No matter how hard he tried, he couldn't get the kiss out of his head. He'd given in to a moment of weakness, but she'd kissed him back. Responded to his touch, yet when it ended, they were like a couple of strangers with each other. He didn't know what to say to her. He loved Rachel with all his heart, and because of that, he'd keep his distance. Leave her alone. She deserved happiness in her life and she wouldn't find it with him.

Though the weather had cleared, so far the store had experienced very little foot traffic.

Shoving aside his heartache, he asked, "Is it normally this slow?" Noah shifted from the window where he'd been staring out at the empty street for some time.

She glanced up from her paperwork. "Sometimes. It depends on the need." For the first time since they'd left the station, she actually smiled at him, a quizzical expression on her pretty face. It took him to the past. He'd always loved the way she looked at him as if she wasn't quite sure what to make of him at times.

He'd made a foolish mistake earlier. Let things become too personal between them. Saving Eva and protecting Rachel required a clear head. Thinking about impossible things was a distraction he couldn't afford.

Noah went to where she worked. "I hate not knowing what's coming next."

She poured a cup of coffee and handed it to him. "It is hard. I wish I could think of something useful. Some explanation why this is happening." She shook her head. "But I don't understand any of it, and I just want Eva home."

He took a sip and sat the cup down. "I still believe we'll bring Eva home safely." The tiniest bit of hope appeared on her face, tugging at his heartstrings. "Do you trust me?" he asked.

"I want to," she murmured, her green eyes huge as she stared into his.

"Then do."

As he looked at her pretty face, doing the right thing felt impossible, but she needed him to be strong for the both of them.

Picking up his coffee, he stepped away, his hands unsteady around the cup. Bitterness resurfaced inside him.

Help me, Lord...

Returning to his perch at the window, regret weighed heavy on his heart. Across the street, something caught his eye. Movement? He squinted past the furniture store to the woods beyond. A glint of something amongst the trees? He couldn't make it out.

He dialed Ryan's number.

"What's up?"

"It may be nothing, but I see something in the woods behind the furniture shop."

"I'm on my way," Ryan said.

Rachel stepped from behind the counter. She'd overheard the call. "Is something wrong?" she asked, her eyes glued to his face.

"I'm not sure." He continued to watch the woods.

The glint flashed again, and it hit him. It was the barrel of a gun. "Get down," he said and dove to get her away from the window.

Crack! In an instant, the window shattered. Scrambling to his feet, he pulled Rachel behind the counter and out of sight.

"Stay down," he warned and unholstered his sidearm, then eased toward the door.

"Ryan, you copy?" Noah asked once he'd redialed.

"Yes. The shot came from behind the store. I'm almost there now. Cole's on the south side of the building. He has eyes on the shooter and is pursuing. I'm on my way to assist," he said through the noise of jostling.

"Copy that." Noah ended the call and hurried to where Rachel crouched.

When he was here last, he noticed a small office to the side of the store. They needed to take cover in case the shooter wasn't acting alone.

He held out his hand. "Come with me. We need someplace secure."

She clasped his hand, and they ran to the windowless office where Noah quickly closed the door. There wasn't a lock. He searched the room for something to secure the door. A desk with a couple of chairs. A file cabinet and a bookcase.

"Help me move the bookcase in front of the door," he told her and grabbed one side while Rachel took the other. Together they shoved the bookcase in front of the door.

"That should at least give them a challenge," he said.

"You don't think this man is alone."

"I'd say the likelihood is slim. I think the shooter is a distraction to draw our backup away."

Reality hit hard and she shivered visibly.

Noah gathered her close. "They'll have to go through me to get to you, and that's not going to happen."

A crashing noise at the rear of the store broke them apart. Noah whirled toward the door. A single set of footsteps. Someone had entered the store.

Being as quiet as possible, Noah called the breach in.

"We're on our way now. The shooter escaped. I'm guessing he was a decoy," Ryan said.

Noah ended the call and shoved the phone in his pocket. "Get behind the desk and stay there no matter what."

With Rachel tucked out of sight, Noah eased to the side of the door. What he heard next was terrifying. Two sets of footsteps nearby. Had the shooter doubled back? While the bookcase would hold them off for a while, it wouldn't take two men long to break through.

Steps halted in front of the door. The knob turned. The door slammed against the bookcase.

"Something is blocking it," a familiar gruff male voice said. It was one of the men who had run them off the road. "Help me out here."

Both men threw their weight against the door. It slammed into the bookcase, swaying it forward. Another blow and it would go over.

Lord, we need Your protection. The prayer slipped through his head as he flattened himself against the wall and called Ryan. "They're inside the store. We need you both right now." Noah heard Ryan confirm they were close.

"Push harder. We need the woman," the same man said. They slammed against the door one more time. The bookcase rocked back and forth before it tumbled forward with a loud crash. The bottom side lodged a few inches from the door, still blocking it.

Thank You, Lord.

The door cracked open. One of the men tried to ease through the sliver. His face was obscured by a ski mask, the attackers' MO from the beginning. Noah pointed his Glock at the man. When he spotted the weapon, he ducked out of sight.

"He's in there with her. Let's get out of here before the others return," the man who'd almost entered the room said. Noah didn't recognize the second man's voice. "I'm not going back to jail because of this. I don't care how much money this guy dangles in front of me to get even with Miller. Let's go."

"Are you nuts? There's two of us. Get out of my way," the familiar voice said. Dressed entirely in black, a mask over his face, the man tried to squeeze through the crack. He had a weapon in his gloved hand. When he spotted Noah, he aimed, but Noah was ready. Firing his weapon, he struck the man's forearm. Somehow the man managed to hold on to his weapon. Noah charged at him. Grabbing the barrel of the gun, he pushed it away. The gun went off, and the bullet sped past Noah's shoulder and lodged in the wall while Noah struggled to get the weapon free.

"Let's go. I hear the other deputies." Footsteps hurried away. The other man was leaving his partner. After a second's hesitation, the first man dropped his weapon, grabbed his injured arm and ran.

Noah tucked the gun in his holster. As much as he wanted to go after them, he wouldn't leave Rachel alone.

Closing the door, he grabbed his phone and called Ryan to tell him the men were leaving through the back entrance.

"We'll see if we can head them off before they get away."

Rachel left her hiding place and rushed to his side. "Did you hear what he said? What do you think he meant when he said he didn't care how much 'this guy' wants to get even with Miller?"

He shook his head. "I don't know, but we need to find out who has a grudge against Allan Miller, and soon."

TWENTY-THREE

A rap on the door sent Rachel jumping. Her heart flew to her throat.

"Noah, it's me." With Rachel's help, Noah was able to push the bookcase out of the way and Cole came in. "Are you two okay?" he asked, glancing from Noah to Rachel.

"We're fine," Noah assured him. "Did you see the two men?"

Cole shook his head. "We traced their footsteps through the woods. I'm sure the shooter had a vehicle waiting there for them. Ryan's following the car tracks in his cruiser."

"I recognized one of the men's voices. He's one of the thugs who ran us off the road. He mentioned something that may be the biggest clue yet." Noah told Cole about the man's comment. Turning to Rachel, he said, "We should get you to the station. It's not safe here."

Shaken by the harrowing experience, her thoughts scattered. "But I will need to do something about the window. We cannot leave it like this."

"We'll put some cardboard across the front for now. I'll call the hardware store in Eagle's Nest and have them come replace the window."

While Noah and Cole taped cardboard on the window, Rachel locked the front door and put out the closed sign.

"That should keep the weather out for now." Noah stood back and surveyed their work before pulling out his phone. "I know the owner of the hardware store, and he owes me a favor. I'll have him stop by after we leave and start the repair."

Rachel couldn't stop shaking. No matter how hard she tried, all she thought about was what the man had said. Was it possible that all of this was because of someone wanting to get even with Allan Miller, and if so, how did she and Eva fit into their plot?

She couldn't get over how familiar Allan Miller seemed. It was too much of a coincidence to be her imagination, but why couldn't she remember how she knew Miller?

"We should go," Noah said and watched her closely. "We can't wait around for the window to be repaired."

She nodded, her troubled thoughts working overtime.

They headed out to the patrol vehicle. The fear spiraling inside her had her glancing around nervously. Noah opened the car door and waited. Their eyes met. He must have seen something in hers because he drew her close and held her for a while. In his strong arms was the only place she honestly felt safe.

She pulled away, her gaze tangling with his. He was so handsome and it broke her heart that they'd been dealt such a cruel blow. She gently touched his cheek, then slipped inside the back seat. A moment passed, and he closed the door and got into the front passenger side.

Cole got behind the wheel and started the engine, pulling out of the alley while Rachel struggled for calm.

With Noah's and Cole's attention on the road ahead, Rachel leaned against the seat and closed her eyes. Exhausted both physically and emotionally, her body craved rest.

Someone gently shook her. Her eyes drifted open, and she stared up at the sheriff's station.

Turning her head, she found Noah watching her. The tenderness on his face made her chest tighten.

"I must have fallen asleep," she murmured, drawing his attention to her mouth. Rachel looked away. They were heading down a dangerous path.

"You're tired," he said, his voice husky. "The sofa in Walker's office is pretty comfortable."

She managed a nod. After another searching look, he opened the door and left the vehicle. While he crossed in front, Rachel covered her warm cheeks with her hands and tried to compose herself. Life could be cruel at times. She and Noah had been kept apart when they were younger by forces out of their control. Now that they'd found each other again, her infertility separated them.

He opened the door and she climbed out next to him. He looked into her eyes without moving. She sensed there were so many things he wanted to say to her. So many things she longed to hear.

"Let's get inside. I don't feel comfortable being out here like this for long."

Reality intruded between them once more and she realized there would never be a right time for them.

Janine met them at the door as if she'd been watching for them. "Are you both okay?" she asked, concerned.

With her heart breaking, it was impossible for Rachel to find words.

"We're fine. It's just been a very long day," Noah said.

"I can imagine. I put on a pot of coffee. It sounds like it's going to be a long night, as well."

"Has something broken on the case?" Noah asked, picking up on the excitement in Janine's voice.

"I'll say. When Aden came on duty, he went to work on finding former employees with a grudge against Allan

Miller, and it sounds like he found someone who was angry enough to want Miller dead."

Noah faced Rachel. As much as he wanted to find out what Aden had discovered, he was worried about her. "Why don't you try and get some rest? I can update you about the case later on."

She shook her head. "This is my family. I can't rest without knowing what's happening."

Her response wasn't a surprise. He clutched her hand and smiled. "All right. Let's go find out."

"Stephanie and I ordered sandwiches. As soon as they arrive we'll bring them in along with the coffee," Janine told them.

Noah stopped and turned back to the woman. "Aren't you supposed to be off duty?"

"Are you kidding? I can't relax until Eva is safely home." She squeezed Rachel's arm.

"Denki," Rachel murmured with heartfelt gratitude.

Walker and Aden were quietly talking when he and Rachel entered the conference room.

"I hear there's been a break in the case," Noah said the minute he stepped inside.

Walker motioned them over. "We believe so. Hargrave sent us the names of some of Miller's former employees. He said after he had time to process what happened to his stepfather, he realized there were several men who had a beef with Miller in the past. One in particular stands out."

Noah peered over Walker's shoulder. "Gary Wilson," he read aloud. "What's his story?"

"For starters, he has a long rap sheet," Aden told him. "Similar to the thugs who attacked you both. Lots of assault and battery charges that landed him in prison for five years. When he was released, Miller gave him a job roughnecking for him. I guess Wilson had some previous experience, and according to Miller's stepson, he always helped out former prisoners. Had a soft spot, I guess."

Walker handed Noah a copy of Wilson's rap sheet. It was lengthy.

"Anyway, it appears Wilson wasn't rehabilitated after all, and it wasn't long before he started stealing from Miller."

Noah's brows slanted together. "Stealing? What type of things?"

"At first, little things, like tools and such. Soon, he graduated to oil rig fittings. He even broke into the office onsite and allegedly stole some money."

"And that's when Miller fired him?" Noah asked.

Aden nodded. "That's right. Miller let him go. According to witnesses, Wilson was furious. He threatened to mess Miller up. The Billings Police Department got called out to remove Wilson from the site, but that's not where it ended."

"Wilson stalked him," Noah supplied, reading the restraining order Miller filed.

"Yep. Miller filed that restraining order because, according to Hargrave, he felt threatened by Wilson."

"I can understand why. This guy has a long history of violence." There was a photo of Wilson's mug shot attached. Noah stared at it, trying to fit the pieces together. He showed the photo to Rachel. "Do you recognize him?"

She studied the picture, then shook her head. "I'm sorry."

"Wilson appears to be in his midtwenties. Do you think this could be the young man Eva was seeing?" Noah asked the occupants of the room.

Walker scratched his head. "It's possible, I guess. I understand this fella had a beef with Miller, but I don't understand how he fits in with Eva or Rachel."

Noah didn't, either. He turned to Aden. "Were there any other incidents after the restraining order was in place?"

Aden studied his laptop. "Nothing that could be substantiated. A couple of letters left in Miller's mailbox…" Aden let out a whistle. "A dead rat on his doorstep with a note reading, 'This is what happens to rats.' Man, this guy is messed up."

"Unbelievable." Noah shook his head. "We're still missing the connection to Rachel and her sister. So assuming Allan Miller is the A. Miller in Eva's note, this ties him to Eva, but it doesn't give us a reason. We have to find out why Miller wanted to meet with her."

"I had Sheriff Solomon ask Beth if she knew an Allan or A. Miller. She said the name was not familiar," Walker said. "I think Eva may be the only one who knows what the connection is at this point."

"Does anyone know where this Wilson person is?" Noah asked.

Walker shook his head. "Not really. His last known address was a vacant lot. The Billings police are looking for him, but no one has seen him in more than a week."

"Around the same time Allan Miller plunged into the lake," Noah said, and all eyes locked onto him.

"According to the records, Wilson never worked on the rig here," Aden said, staring at his laptop screen.

"No, but if he had a grudge against Miller, I'm guessing he was here at some point, watching the man's every move," Noah said.

"See if you can find any sightings of Wilson around town. Let's get some photos printed out and show them to the businesses here and around the Amish community. If he was here, someone had to see him at some point."

"I'm on it," Aden said, and started working on the laptop.

Janine carried in a tray of sandwiches and coffee. "Food's here. Time to refuel."

"Thanks, Janine," Noah acknowledged with a smile as Janine left the room.

Something still troubled him and he couldn't let it go. "Did the police find anything useful at Miller's home?"

"Not a thing," Walker told him. "Everything appeared in order. No signs of a struggle."

Which seemed to indicate Wilson accosted Miller after he left for his hunting trip.

"I think we need to dig deeper into Miller, as well," Noah said on a hunch. "Find out who he associated with and if he had an assistant who might know something about why he was reaching out to Eva."

"That's a good idea. I'll get in touch with the Billings chief of police." Walker grabbed his phone and turned away to make the call.

Noah breathed out a huge sigh. For the first time since this began, he believed they might be able to unravel what was going on.

TWENTY-FOUR

Snow continued to fall harder, blanketing the street in front of the station. An uneasy feeling skipped along Rachel's spine. She couldn't help but believe time was running out for Eva…and her.

"There's been another accident off Mountain Drive." Walker came into the room while putting on his jacket. "A car slid off the road and flipped. I'm heading that way. I'll take Megan with me."

Rachel turned from the window. The second accident in two hours. The weather was really playing havoc with driving.

Megan grabbed her coat and followed the sheriff. With Cole and Ryan dispatched to an earlier accident across town, they were short staffed already.

Rachel didn't miss the worry on Walker's face as he glanced out the window.

"I hate leaving you and Aden here to guard the place, but I'm afraid it can't be helped."

Aden stepped out of the conference room. "Go. Noah and I can handle things here," he assured the sheriff.

Walker cast another troubled look outside. "Let's hope this is the last accident today because we can't afford to send anyone else out on a call." With those troubling words, Walker and Megan headed outside and Janine quickly relocked the door.

She rubbed her arms as she came back. "It's getting colder in here. I'll check the thermostat."

"Any news yet on Wilson's whereabouts?" Noah asked Aden.

"Not yet. I've sent the photo to most of the retail shops around town, but the weather's not helping. A lot of the stores are closing early."

Noah came over to where Rachel stood by the window. "How are you holding up?" he asked quietly.

She forced a smile and faced him. "I'm *oke*."

He appeared exhausted. He'd been through so much for her, suffered injuries to himself just to protect her.

"*Denki*, Noah, for all that you are doing," she said and wondered if she would ever see him again when this ended. It hurt to think there would be no happy-ever-after for them.

"You're welcome." The look in his eyes made it hard not to fall apart. She loved him. He'd always had a place in her heart, yet life wasn't fair.

The weight of the world seemed to be on his shoulders. She touched his cheek. "You are a *gut* man, Noah. I know you blame yourself for what happened with Olivia, but it wasn't your fault. You were just young and rebelling against your *daed*."

He covered her hand with his. "But that doesn't change the truth. A young woman died. Olivia never had the chance to live her life." He stopped and shook his head.

Tears rimmed her eyes. All for him. "Oh, Noah. You must give the pain to *Gott* and let Him bear the burden for you. Pray. Let *Gott* guide you. We all have things we've done wrong. Things we wish had turned out differently. None of us can make up for them by ourselves and you cannot blame yourself forever."

He managed a smile, kissed her hand, and released it.

"I know what you say is true, but it's hard. Letting go of the guilt. Giving it to God completely."

"It is," she agreed. As she looked into his eyes, the lights suddenly extinguished. Rachel sucked in a breath. In the fading afternoon, a scream pierced the shocked silence. Janine. Something had happened to Janine.

"Stay here with Rachel. I'll go check it out." Aden drew his weapon and headed toward the back of the building where the scream had come from.

There'd been no flicker before the lights went out. Almost as if someone had cut the power.

Noah twisted to Rachel. "There's a closet in Walker's office. I need you to go there and hide. Don't come out for anyone but me." He hurried her toward the office.

Noah waited until she was secured in the closet and out of sight before he eased his Glock from its holster and moved to the office door. Aden was nowhere in sight. A tingling of unease lifted the hair on the back of his neck.

"Aden! Janine!" he called out, but there was no answer.

Noah grabbed his cell phone and tried calling Walker. The call went straight to voice mail. Keeping the panic at bay was hard. The area where Walker and Megan were heading was known to have sketchy cell service.

From where he stood, he could see the door to the break room was open. Janine and Aden could be hurt. Noah clicked the lock on the office door and closed it, then made sure the lock had engaged. He slipped to the break room and went inside. Empty.

The hair on the back of his neck stood at attention as he moved toward the restrooms. A search of the men's yielded nothing. He tried to open the door to the ladies' room, but something blocked his way.

Noah shoved hard until he opened the door enough

to enter the room. The lights were off. He flipped the switch, illuminating the room. Janine lay on the floor unconscious. Fear shot through him like a jolt. He knelt beside her and felt for a pulse. She was still alive. She'd been struck by something. He tried to call for backup and an ambulance, but it wouldn't go through. The storm must have been playing havoc on cell service.

A noise close to the rear entrance had him jumping to his feet. He tried the phone again. Still no signal.

Easing from the room, he headed toward the back door. When he drew close, he noticed it stood slightly ajar.

Had Aden heard something outside and gone to investigate? Noah shoved the door the rest of the way open and stepped out into the alley behind the building.

Two cars were parked there that he didn't recognize. He had to get back to Rachel. Noah moved toward the building as his phone rang.

He answered it on first ring thinking it was Aden. "Where are you?"

"I beg your pardon?" Walker.

Noah quickly explained what was happening with an edge to his voice.

"I'll get an ambulance dispatched for Janine. Megan and I are on our way there now. The call was a hoax. There was no accident. I'm guessing these guys wanted us out of the way. Can you see the license plate number on either vehicle? I'll have Megan run it."

Noah read off the license plate of the vehicle in front of him. He'd just recited the last digit when something hard was slammed against his stomach. The breath seeped from his body. He doubled over. Someone shoved him inside.

He landed on his knees. Before he had time to react, another blow struck his injured knee and he dropped to the floor, slamming his shoulder against it. Pain seared through his body. The hand holding the gun felt as if it were weighted down.

Movement nearby. He tried to focus, but it was useless. He was seized from behind. The weapon snatched from his hand.

"I have him. Find her." The man took his phone and smashed it against the floor.

"Get him restrained," a different man said. He recognized the voice.

Noah screamed as his hands were jerked in front of him and zip-tied. Someone pushed him to the floor.

"I have her," another man said. Noah jerked his head behind him and saw a man forcing Rachel along. They'd broken through the locked office door and found her.

Noah tried to struggle to his feet, but someone kicked him in the side, and he slumped to the ground.

"Noah!" He registered the panic in her voice.

"Tie her up. We need to get them out of here. I have no doubt he called for backup." The man who seemed to be running the show was the same one who had run them off the road.

Noah was hauled to his feet and a cover was placed on his head. He couldn't see anything. Where was Rachel? Was she okay?

"What about the other deputy?" the man in charge asked.

"He's taken care of." The answer sent chills down Noah's spine. Aden. Had they killed him? "Get him to the car. We need him to keep her under control."

Someone snatched Noah's arm and forced him out of the station. He was aware of Rachel screaming and he struggled against his captor, but it was useless.

Noah was pushed inside a vehicle. Someone else was thrust in next to him.

A hand touched his arm. Rachel. He folded her hand in his. "It's okay. I'm right here with you."

A sob escaped her. Rachel clutched his hand tight and wouldn't let go.

"What's happening?" she asked in a low voice.

"I'm not sure," he whispered. "But I was able to get one of the license plate numbers to Walker. He's on his way. We have to hang on."

"Keep quiet," the man in charge barked. "You two have caused us enough trouble as it is."

Noah tried to concentrate on the direction he believed the car was heading. They'd turned right. He carefully listened for any sound that might help identify where they were going. The car sped down the road in the opposite direction from which Walker would be approaching. He prayed the license plate wasn't stolen.

After another half hour of driving, the car pulled off the street and headed down what sounded like a gravel road for another couple of miles. The vehicle turned again and slowed to a stop. Rachel clutched Noah's hand tighter.

The door opened, and he was forced to let Rachel go as she was dragged from the car. A few seconds later, someone hauled him from the vehicle and into a dark room whose temperature felt as cold as the outdoors. Someone pushed Noah from behind. He landed on his injured knee again and couldn't hold back the scream. The door shut and locked behind him.

"Noah? Are you here?" Rachel said. He struggled to his feet.

"I'm here." He managed to get the covering from his head. Rachel stood a couple feet away. With his hands restrained, it was hard, but he yanked the covering from Rachel.

A single window allowed silty light through. Someone

huddled in the corner. A woman. She shielded her face as if expecting a blow.

"It's okay, we're not going to hurt you," Noah said. She eased her arms down, and it took him a minute to realize it was Eva. She was alive.

Rachel knelt next to her sister. "I have been so worried," she sobbed.

Eva clung to her, her face bruised, eye swollen. "I am *oke*. I was on my way home when they snatched me. They roughed me up and forced me to go with them. When the car stopped behind me I thought it was…" She stopped.

"You thought it was the young man you were seeing," Rachel answered gently.

Eva's eyes became huge. "How did you know?"

"Anna. She said you were seeing an *Englischer*."

Eva lowered her head. "I'm so sorry," she said through tears. "It was foolish, I know, but I was only having a little fun, and he paid me attention and made me feel special."

"Was it him who took you?" Noah asked. They needed to figure out who these men were working for.

Eva wiped tears from her cheeks. "*Nay*. It was not him. I've not seen these men before."

"You saw their faces?" Noah asked, shocked by the revelation. They hadn't been worried about Eva seeing them, which meant they weren't planning on keeping her alive.

"Eva, who is A. Miller?" Rachel asked.

"How did you know about him?" Eva asked.

Rachel explained how she found the note in the magazine.

"Do you think he is behind this?" Eva couldn't believe it.

"I'm afraid not. Miller's dead, Eva," Noah told her gently.

Eva stared at him in shock, unable to speak for a moment.

"He was such a kind man. I met him at the *shool* one day. He stopped by after class. He said he'd once gone to the *shool*, although I didn't understand since he was *Englisch*. He asked if I would meet him again. I thought it odd, but he seemed nice, so I told him we could meet at the bakery in Eagle's Nest. I wrote it down on a piece of paper and tucked it into the *Blackboard Bulletin* magazine I was reading so I wouldn't forget."

Rachel's brow knitted in a frown. "None of this makes sense. Why did he want to meet with you?"

"He gave me a key and asked me to keep it for him."

"But you didn't meet him at the bakery," Noah said, recalling what the Stoltzfuses said.

Eva shook her head. "*Nay.* He came back to the schoolhouse instead. He appeared frightened when he gave me the key and asked me to hold on to it." She heaved a sigh. "I hid it in the liner of my cloak. When the men took me, they were yelling about him. They were so angry and I worried they'd find it, so when we changed vehicles, I stuffed it under the back seat. Soon after, they brought me here." She shuddered at the memory. "They wouldn't tell me anything. They just dumped me in here. But when they were outside, I heard them discussing that once they had what they needed, they'd make us disappear and no one would be the wiser."

What Eva said confirmed his belief. These men were planning to kill both Rachel and Eva.

"You did well," Noah said, trying to keep his reaction from showing. Whatever the key fit, Noah was sure it would hold all the answers to why this was happening. They just had to stay alive long enough to figure it out.

TWENTY-FIVE

Rachel kept thinking about the photo she'd seen of Allan Miller. A memory from childhood slowly emerged. She was almost positive she'd met Miller when she was young. Before she could figure out the connection, the door rattled. The men had returned. This time, they weren't wearing disguises. They no longer cared if they could be identified.

Rachel recognized one of the men immediately. It was Allan Miller's stepson, Peter Hargrave.

"Peter!" Eva exclaimed, and Rachel spun to her sister in surprise.

"You know this man?" she asked.

"*Jah*, he is the young man who wooed me." The truth finally dawned and tears filled Eva's eyes. She shook her head. "Peter, why are you doing this?"

Hargrave no longer appeared the grieving son.

"Because I have no choice. Can you imagine how surprised I was to learn I wasn't the sole heir to my stepfather's fortunes, that he'd left it all to you two instead?" He pointed an angry finger at Rachel and Eva.

Shock waves rippled through Rachel. What was he talking about?

"I couldn't believe it when I found what appeared to be a copy of the will he'd created leaving almost his entire fortune to a Rachel and Eva Hershberger." Hershberger was Rachel's maiden name before she married Daniel. Either Miller didn't know she'd married, or the will had been made years before she and Daniel wed.

A crazed look appeared on Hargrave's face. "I'd planned things out so carefully. My stepfather's murder was supposed to look like an accident. I'd get his money and pay off McGraff's goons before they could hurt me. But Allan left me the rights to the rig here in Eagle's Nest and nothing more. I was a dead man without that money to pay off my gambling debts."

Rachel couldn't believe what she heard. "Why would he leave his money to us?"

Hargrave scoffed. "Don't try to tell me you didn't know you two were his daughters," he snapped. "It's right there in the letter he sent you. I found it when I searched your place with Mason. I went there to find the original copy of the will, only it wasn't there. So where'd you hide it? If you tell me where it is now, I'll make sure your death is painless."

His words sank in. She and Eva were Miller's daughters? Impossible. Yet memories from her childhood continued to resurface, lending to doubts.

"You'll never get away with it, Hargrave. Even if you do pull off framing Gary Wilson for your stepfather's murder, how will you explain our deaths?" Noah asked.

Rachel couldn't believe how depraved this man was.

Hargrave slowly smiled. "Don't worry, I have ways of making you all disappear, and no one will ever know what happened. The same for Wilson. He'll be gone and won't be able to defend himself against the charges. Case closed."

He stepped closer to Rachel. "Now, where's the original copy of the will? I know you have it." Anger seethed in his eyes.

"I don't know what you're talking about. I've never seen the will."

"You're lying," Hargrave yelled. The man was slipping over the edge and extremely dangerous.

"I'm not. I don't know anything about a will."

Hargrave eyed her for the longest time. With an annoyed sigh, he headed for the door. "You have one hour to tell me the truth before your time is up." Hargrave and his men filed out of the room, slamming the door behind them.

Rachel blew out a breath. "What do we do? I have no idea if there is another copy of the will."

"There has to be. Why else would Mr. Miller leave me a key to protect?" Eva told her. "He said if anything happened to him, I should turn the key in to the sheriff's department."

"He must have suspected something like this would happen and tried to protect you both," Noah said. "Regardless, they're going to kill us. We have to find a way to out of here before they return."

Rachel couldn't believe it. Allan Miller was her father. More childhood memories crowded in. Rachel recalled a man being around when she was younger, but he wasn't her father, or so she'd believed. She remembered Allan Miller's face from long ago. His last name was different back then. She closed her eyes and tried to pull the man out of her memory. She'd heard his surname before. King. His name was King, not Miller.

"I remember him," she said aloud. "I remember Allan Miller. I'd forgotten that there was once another man I'd called *Daed. Mamm* told me he passed away before Eva was born. But his surname was King, not Miller." She looked at Noah.

"Why would he change his name?" Noah asked with a frown.

"I don't know. He appeared quite different back then. Younger, with a beard and hair that was much longer. I have no idea why he left the community and us behind. I remember *Mamm* went through a period of sadness at that time before she met Ezra." She lifted her palms. "Though he wasn't my biological father, Ezra became like a *daed* to me."

Did Miller regret leaving his family behind? Was that why he chose to make her and Eva his heirs?

"I'm guessing Miller did something unlawful, thus the name change," Noah said.

"Why didn't you tell me you received a letter from our father?" Eva asked with hurt in her eyes.

"Because I didn't. I think he sent the letter to *Mamm*." Hargrave had no way of knowing her mother would be able to tell the authorities about the contents of the letter. She prayed he wouldn't realize the truth and go after her *mamm*. Noah moved to the wall opposite the door and examined it. He motioned to Rachel and Eva. "It looks like there's a door behind these boards. It's probably an outside entrance to the basement. If we can get the boards free, we have a chance to escape, but we'll need our hands loose first."

He searched around. "There." He indicated one of the bricks near the door. "I think it's rough enough to saw through these plastic zip ties."

Ignoring the pain in his shoulder, Noah moved his restraints across the sharp edge of the brick. It seemed to take forever before the plastic snapped free. "Rachel, you're next."

Once freed, they quickly began to yank at the boards covering the door. It surprised Rachel how easily they came free, but they were running out of time. Outside the window, darkness settled in.

"Stand back," Noah said. He pulled the last board free of the door. Using all his strength he forced the rusted hinges open.

"Let's get out of here." He grabbed Rachel's hand and she took Eva's as they ran from the basement.

Noah stopped for a moment and glanced around to gain his bearings. "That way." He pointed to the nearby woods. "Whatever happens, don't stop," Noah told them both. "I think I know where we are. This is where Miller stores his drilling equipment. Unfortunately, we're some distance from town, but if we can reach the main highway, perhaps we can flag down someone to help."

They raced for the woods. Behind them, Rachel heard a noise. The men had entered the basement.

"Noah, they're coming," she whispered.

"Keep going," he urged as they ran for their lives.

A shot split the twilight. Hargrave's patience had reached an end. He was shooting to kill. Had he found the original will? She had been so sure they'd find it in whatever the key unlocked, but perhaps she'd been wrong. If he had the will, he didn't need them. Hargrave planned to kill them all and dispose of their bodies where no one would ever find them or Wilson.

Another shot sounded. Noah stumbled and fell to the ground, holding his side. He'd been hit. Rachel ran to him.

"Don't stop," he urged, but she ignored him.

"I'm not leaving you behind." Tears stung her eyes. "Help me, Eva. We need to get out of sight." Rachel put her arm around Noah's waist. With Eva's help, they held him up and stumbled for the woods.

Hiding behind a stand of trees, Rachel struggled to

restrain her labored breathing as several men entered the woods.

Please help us, Gott. The prayer slipped through her thoughts.

No sooner had it ended than Hargrave yelled, "There. I see them. Get them."

"Run," Noah yelled, and they headed deeper into the woods, but the men were almost on top of them.

One man snatched Rachel's arm and forced her away from Noah. Two men grabbed Noah and Eva.

"We have them," one of the men said and shoved Noah hard.

"Noah!" she screamed, so worried about him. Out of the corner of her eye, she saw something flash and prayed it was Noah's team. She glanced his way. He'd seen it, too.

Noah jerked out of his captor's clutches and slugged him hard. The man dropped to the ground, unconscious. He grappled with the man restraining Rachel and slammed his fist against the man's jaw. He fell backward. Eva stomped the foot of the man holding her, and she was free.

"This is Sheriff Collins. You're surrounded, Hargrave. You and your men drop your weapons."

"Get down!" Noah yelled as their assailants opened fire.

Walker and his deputies returned shots, striking one man in the leg. He dropped to the ground clutching the wound. The two men with him fired off more rounds as they ran toward the basement with Cole and Ryan in pursuit.

"Stay low," Noah murmured close to Rachel's ear. He tucked her and Eva near his body as Hargrave's remaining thugs continued shooting at the sheriff's men.

After what felt like a lifetime, the shots faded away. Rachel peeked her head up. The men were surrendering.

"Where's Hargrave?" Rachel asked as she got to her feet and helped Noah up. She looked around and spotted him. "Over there," she said and pointed to the edge of the woods where she saw Hargrave trying to get away.

"Stay here." Noah stumbled to his feet and started after Hargrave, when Megan caught sight of the pursuit and immediately assisted.

"That's far enough. Get your hands in the air," she ordered.

Hargrave froze and slowly raised his hands.

Once the man was cuffed, Megan led him away and Rachel ran to Noah. She'd been so worried.

"You need to have your side checked out. You've lost a lot of blood." She was so worried she'd lose him again.

"It's just a graze." Yet she wasn't convinced. "But I'll let the EMT patch me up," he said with an encouraging smile.

She hugged him close. The tears just wouldn't stop, but it was okay. Eva was safe and Noah was alive and Rachel was ready to take a chance on the future with him...if he would have her.

Rachel waited beside him while the EMT cleaned and bandaged the wound and examined his other injuries. "I don't think you've done any permanent damage to your knee or shoulder."

Walker came over to the ambulance.

"Is there any news on Aden and Janine?" Noah asked.

"They're both okay," Walker quickly assured him. "They took some nasty blows to the head, but they'll be fine."

"That's good to hear. I was worried about them."

"I can't believe this was Hargrave all along. He appeared so innocent." Walker shook his head and addressed Rachel. "I spoke to the former sheriff earlier, because something about Allan Miller didn't add up in my mind. When I showed him the photo we had of Miller, he recognized him right away. Your father changed his name to Miller because he stole some money from someone in the community and worried he'd end up in jail. Miller was a different man then. He made some mistakes, but I believe in the end he tried to make up for them."

She was still in shock. Recalling the father she barely remembered was hard to take in. Rachel had no idea what she and Eva would do with the money he'd left them. Perhaps she could find out who her *daed* stole from and return the money.

But now she was more worried about where she stood with Noah. She loved him. Though different from the love she had for Daniel, a piece of her heart had always belonged to Noah and she didn't want things to end here.

She would tell him her secret and pray it wouldn't cost her his love. But even if he loved her too, would he be willing to leave his life behind and join the Amish as they'd planned so long ago?

"A word." Walker said, and Noah excused himself to follow the sheriff.

"Are you sure you're okay?" Walker asked, though Noah sensed this was not the reason Walker wished to speak to him alone.

"I'm fine. A little banged up, but I'll heal." Noah glanced over to where Rachel stood. He loved her so much. Was this goodbye for them?

"She loves you, too, you know," Walker said quietly as if reading Noah's thoughts.

"Maybe, but it doesn't matter. She deserves someone good. Worthy of her love. She's been through so much."

Walker blew out a breath. "You are good, Noah. I know

you made some mistakes when you were younger, but you were just a kid. It's time you forgave yourself for what happened to Olivia. God has."

Noah swallowed deep. "But I hurt her. I hurt Rachel." His voice was little more than a whisper.

"You were only doing what you thought was best for Rachel because that's what your father wanted you to believe. I don't agree with what he did, but in his own way, he was trying to protect you back then." Walker looked him in the eye, unwavering. "The way I see it, you have two choices. You can walk away from what will probably be the best thing to happen to you, or you can let go of the guilt you've held on to all these years and accept that you have a second chance at happiness." Walker smiled. "I know which one I'd choose." With a pat on his shoulder, Walker left him alone.

Noah couldn't take his eyes off her. He loved her. Didn't want to lose her again. "Please let me be worthy of her love," he whispered and slowly returned to Rachel while praying she would have him.

She stared up at him. He could read all the uncertainty in her eyes.

Noah clasped her hands. "I know I've made a lot of mistakes with you, but one thing has never changed through the years. I love you, Rachel. And I want to spend my life living in the West Kootenai community with you…if you will have me."

Tears filled her eyes. She didn't hesitate. "I love you too, Noah, but there is something you should know."

He frowned at her answer. Another blow was coming. Would it destroy their chance at a future? "What is it?"

It took her a long time to force the words out. "I can't have children," she blurted, then glanced up at him.

Shocked, he wasn't sure he'd heard her correctly. "What do you mean you can't have children?"

Rachel pulled in a breath. "I was pregnant at the time of the accident that took Daniel's life. My injuries were too great. I lost the baby. The doctor said I probably wouldn't be able to have more children, Noah. We would not have babies of our own, and you deserve a family."

His face crumbled, his heart breaking for what she'd been through. "Oh, Rachel." He gathered her close. "I am so sorry about the baby, but don't you know that I love you and want to be with you? I don't care about the rest."

A sob escaped Rachel as she stared up at him with love in her eyes. He lowered his head and kissed her with all the love that had been set free in his heart. He loved her, and they'd work through whatever problems came their way. Together.

She kissed him back and he knew everything would be okay.

"It doesn't matter if we can't have children of our own as long as I have you by my side." He framed her face with his hands. "I love you, Rachel, and I want to marry you and join the Amish faith. I want to live a simple Plain life with you as my wife."

"I want that, too," she whispered, and he kissed her again. He'd loved her all these years never thinking he'd have a second chance to be with her. But God in all His infinite grace had brought them together. Noah was determined nothing would ever tear them apart again. The future and all its happiness soared in front of them like the breathtaking mountains in the distance.

EPILOGUE

One year later...

The door opened. A gust of cold winter air followed Noah inside. Rachel wiped her hands on her apron. She was so nervous, but in a *gut* way. She'd waited all day to tell him her news.

Standing in the doorway, she watched her *mann* shake the snow from his hat and hang it on the peg by the door. He shucked his jacket next and caught her watching him.

Color warmed her cheeks at his smile and the intensity of his gaze on her as he came to her side. Taking her in his arms, Noah kissed her tenderly. Even now, at times, she couldn't believe he was her husband.

After leaving the sheriff's department, Noah had worked so hard to become a member of the community, earning Bishop Aaron's trust, as well as the trust of the Plain people. He told her many times how important joining the church had been for him. Second only to their wedding day.

She recalled that time a year earlier when she'd learned the truth about her biological *daed*. Her *mamm* told her Allan had left her without explanation and filed for divorce soon after. *Mamm* had been distraught at being divorced because she believed she would be shunned by her community, but she'd explained the circumstances to the bishop serving the community at the time and he'd determined

Beth was not at fault. He'd allowed her to marry Ezra and kept Beth's secret, not sharing it with Bishop Aaron when he took over the community.

Rachel had asked her *mamm* why she'd chosen to tell them their father had died. Beth said it was because she didn't want either of her girls to think their *daed* didn't want them when he left her. It took Beth a long time to realize Allan had been a troubled man. As much as Rachel was happy to know her *daed* had reached out to them before his death, in her mind, Ezra would always be the man she thought of as her father.

The key Eva hid in her cloak belonged to a safety deposit box at a bank in Eagle's Nest, where the original will of Allan Miller was found, along with the deed to his home in Billings, and letters to both Rachel and Eva. In them, Allan poured out his heart to his girls and asked for their forgiveness. Both Rachel and Eva willingly gave it.

Though Rachel had asked Noah many times since their life together began, the answer was always the same. He missed nothing about his former time as a deputy. He loved their life together.

"Was iss letz?" Noah asked, his smile disappearing. He must have seen something on her face.

"Nothing is wrong," she quickly assured him. Unable to keep the truth to herself any longer, she blurted out, "I am pregnant, Noah. We are going to have a *boppli*."

She stared up at him, praying he would be as happy as she.

Bemusement shifted to happiness. He lifted her in his arms and swung her around. When he set her down, he kissed her with loving shining in his eyes.

"Are you happy?" she asked, needing to hear him say it.

"Jah, I am happy. I am more than happy. I am blessed. We are going to be parents." He shook his head, won-

derment on his face. "I have all that I've ever dreamed of in you and our Plain life together. And now we will have a child." He buried his face in her neck and wept while she held him close. After she'd lost Noah as a teen, then Daniel's passing, Rachel hadn't been able to imagine being this joyful again. Still, she knew *Gott* had been by her side every step of the way, waiting to bless her with the happiness that only He could give.

* * * * *

If you enjoyed this suspenseful Amish romance,
don't miss Mary Alford's next book,
Amish Country Murder,
available in March 2020
from Love Inspired Suspense!

Find more great reads at
www.LoveInspired.com

Dear Reader,

Sometimes, we are called to move in a different direction in life, even though the possibility is scary and the future unknown.

My seventh Love Inspired Suspense book represents a new direction for me. *Amish Country Kidnapping* is my first Amish romantic suspense, and one that was both a challenge and a blessing to write.

Like me, my hero, Deputy Sheriff Noah Warren, has reached a crossroads in his life. For the longest time, Noah convinced himself he was doing what God wanted of him—until he comes face-to-face with the one woman he never forgot.

Rachel Albrecht still remembers the young boy who stole her heart when she was seventeen, then left her without so much as a word of explanation. But Noah is no longer that carefree young boy. All grown up, he is now the deputy sheriff who rescues Rachel from the hands of her kidnapper, and he is just the hero Rachel needs to help her unravel the secret behind her sister's disappearance.

I hope you enjoyed Noah and Rachel's reunion romance and the struggles they faced along the way. And I hope that their journey to happiness brought a smile to your face.

I love hearing from readers. You can connect with me by visiting my website, www.maryalford.net. Or you can find me on Facebook and Twitter.

All the best,
Mary Alford

WE HOPE YOU ENJOYED THIS BOOK!

Love Inspired SUSPENSE

Uncover the truth in these thrilling
stories of faith in the face of crime
from Love Inspired Suspense.
Discover six new books available
every month, wherever books
are sold!

AVAILABLE THIS MONTH FROM
Love Inspired Suspense

TRAINED TO DEFEND
K-9 Mountain Guardians • by Christy Barritt
Falsely accused of killing her boss, Sarah Peterson has no choice but
to rely on her ex-fiancé, former detective Colton Hawk, and her boss's
loyal husky for protection. But can they clear her name before the real
murderer manages to silence her for good?

AMISH COUNTRY KIDNAPPING
by Mary Alford
For Amish widow Rachel Albrecht, waking up to a man trying to kidnap
her is terrifying—but not as much as discovering he's already taken her
teenaged sister. But when her first love, *Englischer* deputy Noah Warren,
rescues her, can they manage to keep her and her sister alive?

SECRET MOUNTAIN HIDEOUT
by Terri Reed
A witness to murder, Ashley Willis hopes her fake identity will keep
her hidden in a remote mountain town—until she's tracked down by
the killer. Now she has two options: flee again...or allow Deputy Sheriff
Chase Fredrick to guard her.

LONE SURVIVOR
by Jill Elizabeth Nelson
Determined to connect with her last living family member, Karissa Landon
tracks down her cousin—and finds the woman dead and her son a
target. Now going on the run with her cousin's baby boy and firefighter
Hunter Raines may be the only way to survive.

DANGER IN THE DEEP
by Karen Kirst
Aquarium employee Olivia Smith doesn't know why someone wants
her dead—but her deceased husband's friend, Brady Johnson, knows a
secret that could explain it. Brady vowed he'd tell no one his friend had
been on the run from the mob. But could telling Olivia save her life?

COLORADO MANHUNT
by Lisa Phillips and Jenna Night
The hunt for fugitives turns deadly in these two thrilling novellas, where
a US marshal must keep a witness safe after the brother she testified
against escapes prison, and a bounty hunter discovers she and the
vicious gang after her bail jumper tracked the man's twin instead.

Get 4 FREE REWARDS!

We'll send you 2 FREE Books plus 2 FREE Mystery Gifts.

Love Inspired® Suspense books feature Christian characters facing challenges to their faith... and lives.

FREE Value Over $20

YES! Please send me 2 FREE Love Inspired® Suspense novels and my 2 FREE mystery gifts (gifts are worth about $10 retail). After receiving them, if I don't wish to receive any more books, I can return the shipping statement marked "cancel." If I don't cancel, I will receive 6 brand-new novels every month and be billed just $5.24 each for the regular-print edition or $5.99 each for the larger-print edition in the U.S., or $5.74 each for the regular-print edition or $6.24 each for the larger-print edition in Canada. That's a savings of at least 13% off the cover price. It's quite a bargain! Shipping and handling is just 50¢ per book in the U.S. and $1.25 per book in Canada.* I understand that accepting the 2 free books and gifts places me under no obligation to buy anything. I can always return a shipment and cancel at any time. The free books and gifts are mine to keep no matter what I decide.

Choose one: ☐ **Love Inspired® Suspense Regular-Print** (153/353 IDN GNWN)   ☐ **Love Inspired® Suspense Larger-Print** (107/307 IDN GNWN)

Name (please print)

Address   Apt. #

City   State/Province   Zip/Postal Code

Mail to the **Reader Service:**
IN U.S.A.: P.O. Box 1341, Buffalo, NY 14240-8531
IN CANADA: P.O. Box 603, Fort Erie, Ontario L2A 5X3

Want to try 2 free books from another series! Call 1-800-873-8635 or visit www.ReaderService.com.
